Samuel Langhorne Clemens (November 30, 1835 – April 21, 1910), known by his pen name Mark Twain, was an American writer, humorist, entrepreneur, publisher, and lecturer. He was lauded as the "greatest humorist this country has produced", and William Faulkner called him "the father of American literature". His novels include The Adventures of Tom Sawyer (1876) and its sequel, the Adventures of Huckleberry Finn (1884), the latter often called "The Great American Novel".

Twain was raised in Hannibal, Missouri, which later provided the setting for Tom Sawyer and Huckleberry Finn. He served an apprenticeship with a printer and then worked as a typesetter, contributing articles to the newspaper of his older brother Orion Clemens. He later became a riverboat pilot on the Mississippi River before heading west to join Orion in Nevada. (Source: Wikipedia)

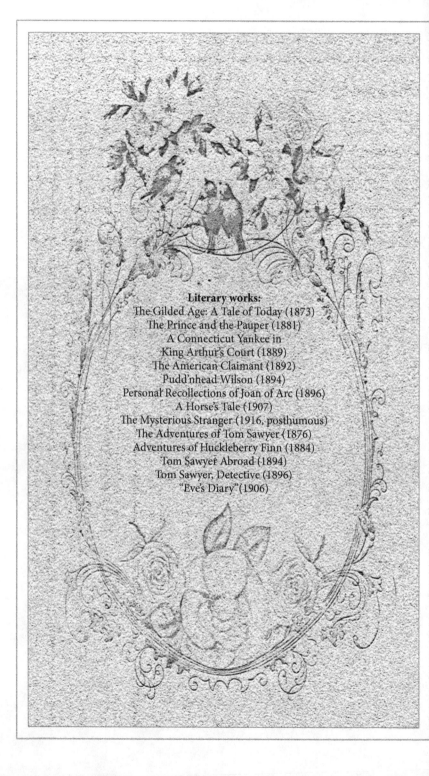

Literary works:
The Gilded Age: A Tale of Today (1873)
The Prince and the Pauper (1881)
A Connecticut Yankee in
King Arthur's Court (1889)
The American Claimant (1892)
Pudd'nhead Wilson (1894)
Personal Recollections of Joan of Arc (1896)
A Horse's Tale (1907)
The Mysterious Stranger (1916, posthumous)
The Adventures of Tom Sawyer (1876)
Adventures of Huckleberry Finn (1884)
Tom Sawyer Abroad (1894)
Tom Sawyer, Detective (1896)
"Eve's Diary" (1906)

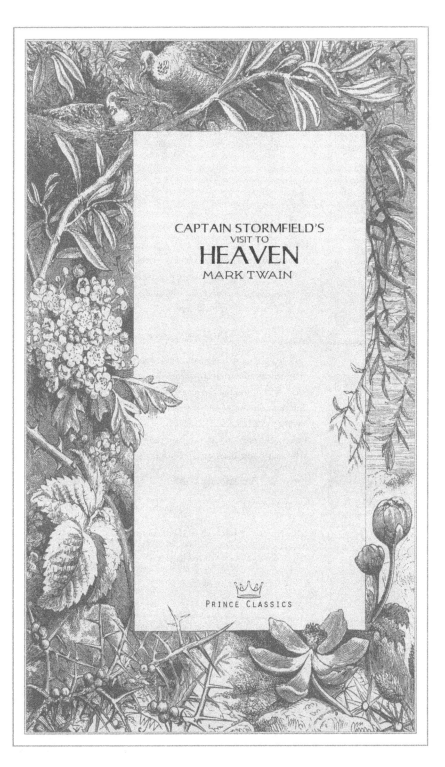

CAPTAIN STORMFIELD'S
VISIT TO
HEAVEN

MARK TWAIN

PRINCE CLASSICS

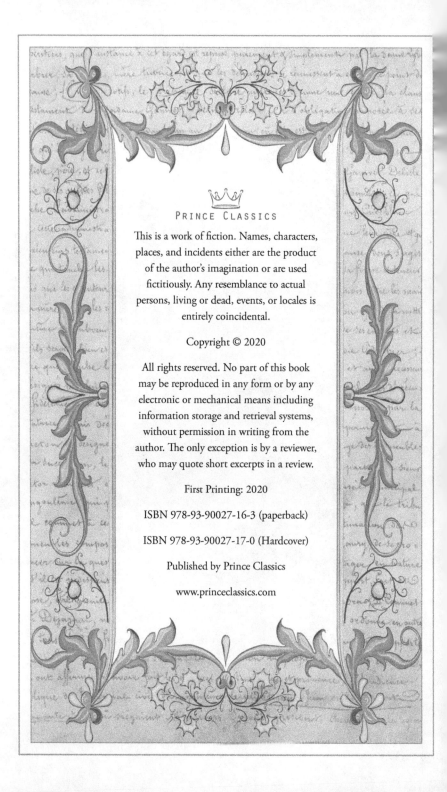

PRINCE CLASSICS

First Printing: 2020

ISBN 978-93-90027-16-3 (paperback)

ISBN 978-93-90027-17-0 (Hardcover)

Published by Prince Classics

www.princeclassics.com

Contents

CAPTAIN STORMFIELD'S
VISIT TO
HEAVEN

CHAPTER I

Well, when I had been dead about thirty years I begun to get a little anxious. Mind you, had been whizzing through space all that time, like a comet. *Like* a comet! Why, Peters, I laid over the lot of them! Of course there warn't any of them going my way, as a steady thing, you know, because they travel in a long circle like the loop of a lasso, whereas I was pointed as straight as a dart for the Hereafter; but I happened on one every now and then that was going my way for an hour or so, and then we had a bit of a brush together. But it was generally pretty one-sided, because I sailed by them the same as if they were standing still. An ordinary comet don't make more than about 200,000 miles a minute. Of course when I came across one of that sort—like Encke's and Halley's comets, for instance—it warn't anything but just a flash and a vanish, you see. You couldn't rightly call it a race. It was as if the comet was a gravel-train and I was a telegraph despatch. But after I got outside of our astronomical system, I used to flush a comet occasionally that was something *like*. *We* haven't got any such comets—ours don't begin. One night I was swinging along at a good round gait, everything taut and trim, and the wind in my favor—I judged I was going about a million miles a minute—it might have been more, it couldn't have been less—when I flushed a most uncommonly big one about three points off my starboard bow. By his stern lights I judged he was bearing about northeast-and-by-north-half-east. Well, it was so near my course that I wouldn't throw away the chance; so I fell off a point, steadied my helm, and went for him. You should have heard me whiz, and seen the electric fur fly! In about a minute and a half I was fringed out with an electrical nimbus that flamed around for miles and miles and lit up all space like broad day. The comet was burning blue in the distance, like a sickly torch, when I first sighted him, but he begun to grow bigger and bigger as I crept up on him. I slipped up on him so fast that when I had gone about 150,000,000 miles I was close enough to be swallowed up in the phosphorescent glory of his wake, and I couldn't see anything for the glare. Thinks I, it won't do to run into him, so I shunted to one side and tore along.

By and by I closed up abreast of his tail. Do you know what it was like? It was like a gnat closing up on the continent of America. I forged along. By and by I had sailed along his coast for a little upwards of a hundred and fifty million miles, and then I could see by the shape of him that I hadn't even got up to his waistband yet. Why, Peters, *we* don't know anything about comets, down here. If you want to see comets that *are* comets, you've got to go outside of our solar system—where there's room for them, you understand. My friend, I've seen comets out there that couldn't even lay down inside the *orbits* of our noblest comets without their tails hanging over.

Well, I boomed along another hundred and fifty million miles, and got up abreast his shoulder, as you may say. I was feeling pretty fine, I tell you; but just then I noticed the officer of the deck come to the side and hoist his glass in my direction. Straight off I heard him sing out—"Below there, ahoy! Shake her up, shake her up! Heave on a hundred million billion tons of brimstone!"

"Ay-ay, sir!"

"Pipe the stabboard watch! All hands on deck!"

"Ay-ay, sir!"

"Send two hundred thousand million men aloft to shake out royals and sky-scrapers!"

"Ay-ay, sir!"

"Hand the stuns'ls! Hang out every rag you've got! Clothe her from stem to rudder-post!"

"Ay-ay, sir!"

In about a second I begun to see I'd woke up a pretty ugly customer, Peters. In less than ten seconds that comet was just a blazing cloud of red-hot canvas. It was piled up into the heavens clean out of sight—the old thing seemed to swell out and occupy all space; the sulphur smoke from the furnaces—oh, well, nobody can describe the way it rolled and tumbled up into the skies, and nobody can half describe the way it smelt. Neither can anybody begin to describe the way that monstrous craft begun to crash along. And such another powwow—thousands of bo's'n's whistles screaming at once, and a crew like the populations of a hundred thousand worlds like ours all swearing at once. Well, I never heard the like of it before.

We roared and thundered along side by side, both doing our level best, because I'd never struck a comet before that could lay over me, and so I was bound to beat this one or break something. I judged I had some reputation in space, and I calculated to keep it. I noticed I wasn't gaining as fast, now, as I was before, but still I was gaining. There was a power of excitement on board the comet. Upwards of a hundred billion passengers swarmed up from below and rushed to the side and begun to bet on the race. Of course this careened her and damaged her speed. My, but wasn't the mate mad! He jumped at that crowd, with his trumpet in his hand, and sung out—

"Amidships! amidships, you—! [9] or I'll brain the last idiot of you!"

Well, sir, I gained and gained, little by little, till at last I went skimming sweetly by the magnificent old conflagration's nose. By this time the captain of the comet had been rousted out, and he stood there in the red glare for'ard, by the mate, in his shirt-sleeves and slippers, his hair all rats' nests and one suspender hanging, and how sick those two men did look! I just simply couldn't help putting my thumb to my nose as I glided away and singing out:

"Ta-ta! ta-ta! Any word to send to your family?"

Peters, it was a mistake. Yes, sir, I've often regretted that—it was a mistake. You see, the captain had given up the race, but that remark was too tedious for him—he couldn't stand it. He turned to the mate, and says he—

"Have we got brimstone enough of our own to make the trip?"

"Yes, sir."

"Sure?"

"Yes, sir—more than enough."

"How much have we got in cargo for Satan?"

"Eighteen hundred thousand billion quintillions of kazarks."

"Very well, then, let his boarders freeze till the next comet comes. Lighten ship! Lively, now, lively, men! Heave the whole cargo overboard!"

Peters, look me in the eye, and be calm. I found out, over there, that a kazark is exactly the bulk of a *hundred and sixty-nine worlds like ours!* They hove all that load overboard. When it fell it wiped out a considerable raft of stars just as clean as if they'd been candles and somebody blowed them out. As for the race, that was at an end. The minute she was lightened the comet swung along by me the same as if I was anchored. The captain stood on the stern, by the after-davits, and put his thumb to his nose and sung out—

"Ta-ta! ta-ta! Maybe *you've* got some message to send your friends in the Everlasting Tropics!"

Then he hove up his other suspender and started for'ard, and inside of three-quarters of an hour his craft was only a pale torch again in the distance. Yes, it was a mistake, Peters—that remark of mine. I don't reckon I'll ever get over being sorry about it. I'd 'a' beat the bully of the firmament if I'd kept my mouth shut.

But I've wandered a little off the track of my tale; I'll get back on my course again. Now you see what kind of speed I was making. So, as I said, when I had been tearing along this way about thirty years I begun to get uneasy. Oh, it was pleasant enough, with a good deal to find out, but then it was kind of lonesome, you know. Besides, I wanted to get somewhere. I hadn't shipped with the idea of cruising forever. First off, I liked the delay, because I judged I was going to fetch up in pretty warm quarters when I got through; but towards the last I begun to feel that I'd rather go to—well, most any place, so as to finish up the uncertainty.

Well, one night—it was always night, except when I was rushing by some star that was occupying the whole universe with its fire and its glare—light enough then, of course, but I necessarily left it behind in a minute or two and plunged into a solid week of darkness again. The stars ain't so close together as they look to be. Where was I? Oh yes; one night I was sailing along, when I discovered a tremendous long row of blinking lights away on the horizon ahead. As I approached, they begun to tower and swell and look like mighty furnaces. Says I to myself—

"By George, I've arrived at last—and at the wrong place, just as I expected!"

Then I fainted. I don't know how long I was insensible, but it must have been a good while, for, when I came to, the darkness was all gone and there was the loveliest sunshine and the balmiest, fragrantest air in its place. And there was such a marvellous world spread out before me—such a glowing, beautiful, bewitching country. The things I took for furnaces were gates, miles high, made all of flashing jewels, and they pierced a wall of solid gold that you couldn't see the top of, nor yet the end of, in either direction. I was pointed straight for one of these gates, and a-coming like a house afire. Now I noticed that the skies were black with millions of people, pointed for those gates. What a roar they made, rushing through the air! The ground was as thick as ants with people, too—billions of them, I judge.

I lit. I drifted up to a gate with a swarm of people, and when it was my turn the head clerk says, in a business-like way—

"Well, quick! Where are you from?"

"San Francisco," says I.

"San Fran—*what?*" says he.

"San Francisco."

He scratched his head and looked puzzled, then he says—

"Is it a planet?"

By George, Peters, think of it! *"Planet?"* says I; "it's a city. And moreover, it's one of the biggest and finest and—"

"There, there!" says he, "no time here for conversation. We don't deal in cities here. Where are you from in a *general* way?"

"Oh," I says, "I beg your pardon. Put me down for California."

I had him *again*, Peters! He puzzled a second, then he says, sharp and irritable—

"I don't know any such planet—is it a constellation?"

"Oh, my goodness!" says I. "Constellation, says you? No—it's a State."

"Man, we don't deal in States here. *Will* you tell me where you are from *in general—at large*, don't you understand?"

"Oh, now I get your idea," I says. "I'm from America,—the United States of America."

Peters, do you know I had him *again*? If I hadn't I'm a clam! His face was as blank as a target after a militia shooting-match. He turned to an under clerk and says—

"Where is America? *What* is America?"

The under clerk answered up prompt and says—

"There ain't any such orb."

"*Orb*?" says I. "Why, what are you talking about, young man? It ain't an orb; it's a country; it's a continent. Columbus discovered it; I reckon likely you've heard of *him*, anyway. America—why, sir, America—"

"Silence!" says the head clerk. "Once for all, where—are—you—*from*?"

"Well," says I, "I don't know anything more to say—unless I lump things, and just say I'm from the world."

"Ah," says he, brightening up, "now that's something like! *What* world?"

Peters, he had *me*, that time. I looked at him, puzzled, he looked at me, worried. Then he burst out—

"Come, come, what world?"

Says I, "Why, *the* world, of course."

"*The* world!" he says. "H'm! there's billions of them! . . . Next!"

That meant for me to stand aside. I done so, and a sky-blue man with seven heads and only one leg hopped into my place. I took a walk. It just occurred to me, then, that all the myriads I had seen swarming to that gate, up to this time, were just like that creature. I tried to run across somebody I was acquainted with, but they were out of acquaintances of mine just then. So I thought the thing all over and finally sidled back there pretty meek and feeling rather stumped, as you may say.

"Well?" said the head clerk.

"Well, sir," I says, pretty humble, "I don't seem to make out which world it is I'm from. But you may know it from this—it's the one the Saviour saved."

He bent his head at the Name. Then he says, gently—

"The worlds He has saved are like to the gates of heaven in number—none can count them. What astronomical system is your world in?—perhaps that may assist."

"It's the one that has the sun in it—and the moon—and Mars"—he shook his head at each name—hadn't ever heard of them, you see—"and Neptune—and Uranus—and Jupiter—"

"Hold on!" says he—"hold on a minute! Jupiter . . . Jupiter . . . Seems to me we had a man from there eight or nine hundred years ago—but people from that system very seldom enter by this gate." All of a sudden he begun to look me so straight in the eye that I thought he was going to bore through me. Then he says, very deliberate, "Did you come *straight here* from your system?"

"Yes, sir," I says—but I blushed the least little bit in the world when I said it.

He looked at me very stern, and says—

"That is not true; and this is not the place for prevarication. You wandered from your course. How did that happen?"

15

Says I, blushing again—

"I'm sorry, and I take back what I said, and confess. I raced a little with a comet one day—only just the least little bit—only the tiniest lit—"

"So—so," says he—and without any sugar in his voice to speak of.

I went on, and says—

"But I only fell off just a bare point, and I went right back on my course again the minute the race was over."

"No matter—that divergence has made all this trouble. It has brought you to a gate that is billions of leagues from the right one. If you had gone to your own gate they would have known all about your world at once and there would have been no delay. But we will try to accommodate you." He turned to an under clerk and says—

"What system is Jupiter in?"

"I don't remember, sir, but I think there is such a planet in one of the little new systems away out in one of the thinly worlded corners of the universe. I will see."

He got a balloon and sailed up and up and up, in front of a map that was as big as Rhode Island. He went on up till he was out of sight, and by and by he came down and got something to eat and went up again. To cut a long story short, he kept on doing this for a day or two, and finally he came down and said he thought he had found that solar system, but it might be fly-specks. So he got a microscope and went back. It turned out better than he feared. He had rousted out our system, sure enough. He got me to describe our planet and its distance from the sun, and then he says to his chief—

"Oh, I know the one he means, now, sir. It is on the map. It is called the Wart."

Says I to myself, "Young man, it wouldn't be wholesome for you to go down *there* and call it the Wart."

Well, they let me in, then, and told me I was safe forever and wouldn't have any more trouble.

16

Then they turned from me and went on with their work, the same as if they considered my case all complete and shipshape. I was a good deal surprised at this, but I was diffident about speaking up and reminding them. I did so hate to do it, you know; it seemed a pity to bother them, they had so much on their hands. Twice I thought I would give up and let the thing go; so twice I started to leave, but immediately I thought what a figure I should cut stepping out amongst the redeemed in such a rig, and that made me hang back and come to anchor again. People got to eying me—clerks, you know—wondering why I didn't get under way. I couldn't stand this long—it was too uncomfortable. So at last I plucked up courage and tipped the head clerk a signal. He says—

"What! you here yet? What's wanting?"

Says I, in a low voice and very confidential, making a trumpet with my hands at his ear—

"I beg pardon, and you mustn't mind my reminding you, and seeming to meddle, but hain't you forgot something?"

He studied a second, and says—

"Forgot something? . . . No, not that I know of."

"Think," says I.

He thought. Then he says—

"No, I can't seem to have forgot anything. What is it?"

"Look at me," says I, "look me all over."

He done it.

"Well?" says he.

"Well," says I, "you don't notice anything? If I branched out amongst the elect looking like this, wouldn't I attract considerable attention?—wouldn't I be a little conspicuous?"

"Well," he says, "I don't see anything the matter. What do you lack?"

"Lack! Why, I lack my harp, and my wreath, and my halo, and my hymn-book, and my palm branch—I lack everything that a body naturally requires up here, my friend."

Puzzled? Peters, he was the worst puzzled man you ever saw. Finally he says—

"Well, you seem to be a curiosity every way a body takes you. I never heard of these things before."

I looked at the man awhile in solid astonishment; then I says—

"Now, I hope you don't take it as an offence, for I don't mean any, but really, for a man that has been in the Kingdom as long as I reckon you have, you do seem to know powerful little about its customs."

"Its customs!" says he. "Heaven is a large place, good friend. Large empires have many and diverse customs. Even small dominions have, as you doubtless know by what you have seen of the matter on a small scale in the Wart. How can you imagine I could ever learn the varied customs of the countless kingdoms of heaven? It makes my head ache to think of it. I know the customs that prevail in those portions inhabited by peoples that are appointed to enter by my own gate—and hark ye, that is quite enough knowledge for one individual to try to pack into his head in the thirty-seven millions of years I have devoted night and day to that study. But the idea of learning the customs of the whole appalling expanse of heaven—O man, how insanely you talk! Now I don't doubt that this odd costume you talk about is the fashion in that district of heaven you belong to, but you won't be conspicuous in this section without it."

I felt all right, if that was the case, so I bade him good-day and left. All day I walked towards the far end of a prodigious hall of the office, hoping to come out into heaven any moment, but it was a mistake. That hall was built on the general heavenly plan—it naturally couldn't be small. At last I got so tired I couldn't go any farther; so I sat down to rest, and begun to tackle the queerest sort of strangers and ask for information, but I didn't get any; they couldn't understand my language, and I could not understand theirs. I got dreadfully lonesome. I was so down-hearted and homesick I wished a hundred times I never had died. I turned back, of course. About noon next day, I got back at last and was on hand at the booking-office once more. Says I to the head clerk—

"I begin to see that a man's got to be in his own Heaven to be happy."

"Perfectly correct," says he. "Did you imagine the same heaven would suit all sorts of men?"

"Well, I had that idea—but I see the foolishness of it. Which way am I to go to get to my district?"

He called the under clerk that had examined the map, and he gave me general directions. I thanked him and started; but he says—

"Wait a minute; it is millions of leagues from here. Go outside and stand on that red wishing-carpet; shut your eyes, hold your breath, and wish yourself there."

"I'm much obliged," says I; "why didn't you dart me through when I first arrived?"

"We have a good deal to think of here; it was your place to think of it and ask for it. Good-by; we probably sha'n't see you in this region for a thousand centuries or so."

"In that case, *o revoor*," says I.

I hopped onto the carpet and held my breath and shut my eyes and wished I was in the booking-office of my own section. The very next instant a voice I knew sung out in a business kind of a way—

"A harp and a hymn-book, pair of wings and a halo, size 13, for Cap'n Eli Stormfield, of San Francisco!—make him out a clean bill of health, and let him in."

I opened my eyes. Sure enough, it was a Pi Ute Injun I used to know in Tulare County; mighty good fellow—I remembered being at his funeral, which consisted of him being burnt and the other Injuns gauming their faces

19

with his ashes and howling like wildcats. He was powerful glad to see me, and you may make up your mind I was just as glad to see him, and feel that I was in the right kind of a heaven at last.

Just as far as your eye could reach, there was swarms of clerks, running and bustling around, tricking out thousands of Yanks and Mexicans and English and Arabs, and all sorts of people in their new outfits; and when they gave me my kit and I put on my halo and took a look in the glass, I could have jumped over a house for joy, I was so happy. "Now *this* is something like!" says I. "Now," says I, "I'm all right—show me a cloud."

Inside of fifteen minutes I was a mile on my way towards the cloud-banks and about a million people along with me. Most of us tried to fly, but some got crippled and nobody made a success of it. So we concluded to walk, for the present, till we had had some wing practice.

We begun to meet swarms of folks who were coming back. Some had harps and nothing else; some had hymn-books and nothing else; some had nothing at all; all of them looked meek and uncomfortable; one young fellow hadn't anything left but his halo, and he was carrying that in his hand; all of a sudden he offered it to me and says—

"Will you hold it for me a minute?"

Then he disappeared in the crowd. I went on. A woman asked me to hold her palm branch, and then *she* disappeared. A girl got me to hold her harp for her, and by George, *she* disappeared; and so on and so on, till I was about loaded down to the guards. Then comes a smiling old gentleman and asked me to hold *his* things. I swabbed off the perspiration and says, pretty tart—

"I'll have to get you to excuse me, my friend,—*I* ain't no hat-rack."

About this time I begun to run across piles of those traps, lying in the road. I just quietly dumped my extra cargo along with them. I looked around, and, Peters, that whole nation that was following me were loaded down the same as I'd been. The return crowd had got them to hold their things a minute, you see. They all dumped their loads, too, and we went on.

When I found myself perched on a cloud, with a million other people, I never felt so good in my life. Says I, "Now this is according to the promises; I've been having my doubts, but now I am in heaven, sure enough." I gave my palm branch a wave or two, for luck, and then I tautened up my harp-strings and struck in. Well, Peters, you can't imagine anything like the row we made. It was grand to listen to, and made a body thrill all over, but there was considerable many tunes going on at once, and that was a drawback to the harmony, you understand; and then there was a lot of Injun tribes, and they kept up such another war-whooping that they kind of took the tuck out of the music. By and by I quit performing, and judged I'd take a rest. There was quite a nice mild old gentleman sitting next me, and I noticed he didn't take a hand; I encouraged him, but he said he was naturally bashful, and was afraid to try before so many people. By and by the old gentleman said he never could seem to enjoy music somehow. The fact was, I was beginning to feel the same way; but I didn't say anything. Him and I had a considerable long silence, then, but of course it warn't noticeable in that place. After about sixteen or seventeen hours, during which I played and sung a little, now and then—always the same tune, because I didn't know any other—I laid down my harp and begun to fan myself with my palm branch. Then we both got to sighing pretty regular. Finally, says he—

"Don't you know any tune but the one you've been pegging at all day?"

"Not another blessed one," says I.

"Don't you reckon you could learn another one?" says he.

"Never," says I; "I've tried to, but I couldn't manage it."

"It's a long time to hang to the one—eternity, you know."

"Don't break my heart," says I; "I'm getting low-spirited enough already."

After another long silence, says he—

"Are you glad to be here?"

Says I, "Old man, I'll be frank with you. This *ain't* just as near my idea of bliss as I thought it was going to be, when I used to go to church."

21

Says he, "What do you say to knocking off and calling it half a day?"

"That's me," says I. "I never wanted to get off watch so bad in my life."

So we started. Millions were coming to the cloud-bank all the time, happy and hosannahing; millions were leaving it all the time, looking mighty quiet, I tell you. We laid for the new-comers, and pretty soon I'd got them to hold all my things a minute, and then I was a free man again and most outrageously happy. Just then I ran across old Sam Bartlett, who had been dead a long time, and stopped to have a talk with him. Says I—

"Now tell me—is this to go on forever? Ain't there anything else for a change?"

Says he—

"I'll set you right on that point very quick. People take the figurative language of the Bible and the allegories for literal, and the first thing they ask for when they get here is a halo and a harp, and so on. Nothing that's harmless and reasonable is refused a body here, if he asks it in the right spirit. So they are outfitted with these things without a word. They go and sing and play just about one day, and that's the last you'll ever see them in the choir. They don't need anybody to tell them that that sort of thing wouldn't make a heaven—at least not a heaven that a sane man could stand a week and remain sane. That cloud-bank is placed where the noise can't disturb the old inhabitants, and so there ain't any harm in letting everybody get up there and cure himself as soon as he comes.

"Now you just remember this—heaven is as blissful and lovely as it can be; but it's just the busiest place you ever heard of. There ain't any idle people here after the first day. Singing hymns and waving palm branches through all eternity is pretty when you hear about it in the pulpit, but it's as poor a way to put in valuable time as a body could contrive. It would just make a heaven of warbling ignoramuses, don't you see? Eternal Rest sounds comforting in the pulpit, too. Well, you try it once, and see how heavy time will hang on your hands. Why, Stormfield, a man like you, that had been active and stirring all his life, would go mad in six months in a heaven where he hadn't anything to do. Heaven is the very last place to come to *rest* in,—and don't you be afraid to bet on that!"

Says I—

"Sam, I'm as glad to hear it as I thought I'd be sorry. I'm glad I come, now."

Says he—

"Cap'n, ain't you pretty physically tired?"

Says I—

"Sam, it ain't any name for it! I'm dog-tired."

"Just so—just so. You've earned a good sleep, and you'll get it. You've earned a good appetite, and you'll enjoy your dinner. It's the same here as it is on earth—you've got to earn a thing, square and honest, before you enjoy it. You can't enjoy first and earn afterwards. But there's this difference, here: you can choose your own occupation, and all the powers of heaven will be put forth to help you make a success of it, if you do your level best. The shoemaker on earth that had the soul of a poet in him won't have to make shoes here."

"Now that's all reasonable and right," says I. "Plenty of work, and the kind you hanker after; no more pain, no more suffering—"

"Oh, hold on; there's plenty of pain here—but it don't kill. There's plenty of suffering here, but it don't last. You see, happiness ain't a *thing in itself*—it's only a *contrast* with something that ain't pleasant. That's all it is. There ain't a thing you can mention that is happiness in its own self—it's only so by contrast with the other thing. And so, as soon as the novelty is over and the force of the contrast dulled, it ain't happiness any longer, and you have to get something fresh. Well, there's plenty of pain and suffering in heaven— consequently there's plenty of contrasts, and just no end of happiness."

Says I, "It's the sensiblest heaven I've heard of yet, Sam, though it's about as different from the one I was brought up on as a live princess is different from her own wax figger."

23

Along in the first months I knocked around about the Kingdom, making friends and looking at the country, and finally settled down in a pretty likely region, to have a rest before taking another start. I went on making acquaintances and gathering up information. I had a good deal of talk with an old bald-headed angel by the name of Sandy McWilliams. He was from somewhere in New Jersey. I went about with him, considerable. We used to lay around, warm afternoons, in the shade of a rock, on some meadow-ground that was pretty high and out of the marshy slush of his cranberry-farm, and there we used to talk about all kinds of things, and smoke pipes. One day, says I—

"About how old might you be, Sandy?"

"Seventy-two."

"I judged so. How long you been in heaven?"

"Twenty-seven years, come Christmas."

"How old was you when you come up?"

"Why, seventy-two, of course."

"You can't mean it!"

"Why can't I mean it?"

"Because, if you was seventy-two then, you are naturally ninety-nine now."

"No, but I ain't. I stay the same age I was when I come."

"Well," says I, "come to think, there's something just here that I want to ask about. Down below, I always had an idea that in heaven we would all be young, and bright, and spry."

"Well, you can be young if you want to. You've only got to wish."

"Well, then, why didn't you wish?"

"I did. They all do. You'll try it, some day, like enough; but you'll get tired of the change pretty soon."

"Why?"

"Well, I'll tell you. Now you've always been a sailor; did you ever try some other business?"

"Yes, I tried keeping grocery, once, up in the mines; but I couldn't stand it; it was too dull—no stir, no storm, no life about it; it was like being part dead and part alive, both at the same time. I wanted to be one thing or t'other. I shut up shop pretty quick and went to sea."

"That's it. Grocery people like it, but you couldn't. You see you wasn't used to it. Well, I wasn't used to being young, and I couldn't seem to take any interest in it. I was strong, and handsome, and had curly hair,—yes, and wings, too!—gay wings like a butterfly. I went to picnics and dances and parties with the fellows, and tried to carry on and talk nonsense with the girls, but it wasn't any use; I couldn't take to it—fact is, it was an awful bore. What I wanted was early to bed and early to rise, and something to *do*; and when my work was done, I wanted to sit quiet, and smoke and think—not tear around with a parcel of giddy young kids. You can't think what I suffered whilst I was young."

"How long was you young?"

"Only two weeks. That was plenty for me. Laws, I was so lonesome! You see, I was full of the knowledge and experience of seventy-two years; the deepest subject those young folks could strike was only *a-b-c* to me. And to hear them argue—oh, my! it would have been funny, if it hadn't been so pitiful. Well, I was so hungry for the ways and the sober talk I was used to, that I tried to ring in with the old people, but they wouldn't have it. They considered me a conceited young upstart, and gave me the cold shoulder. Two weeks was a-plenty for me. I was glad to get back my bald head again, and my pipe, and my old drowsy reflections in the shade of a rock or a tree."

"Well," says I, "do you mean to say you're going to stand still at seventy-two, forever?"

"I don't know, and I ain't particular. But I ain't going to drop back to twenty-five any more—I know that, mighty well. I know a sight more than

I did twenty-seven years ago, and I enjoy learning, all the time, but I don't seem to get any older. That is, bodily—my mind gets older, and stronger, and better seasoned, and more satisfactory."

Says I, "If a man comes here at ninety, don't he ever set himself back?"

"Of course he does. He sets himself back to fourteen; tries it a couple of hours, and feels like a fool; sets himself forward to twenty; it ain't much improvement; tries thirty, fifty, eighty, and finally ninety—finds he is more at home and comfortable at the same old figure he is used to than any other way. Or, if his mind begun to fail him on earth at eighty, that's where he finally sticks up here. He sticks at the place where his mind was last at its best, for there's where his enjoyment is best, and his ways most set and established."

"Does a chap of twenty-five stay always twenty-five, and look it?"

"If he is a fool, yes. But if he is bright, and ambitious and industrious, the knowledge he gains and the experiences he has, change his ways and thoughts and likings, and make him find his best pleasure in the company of people above that age; so he allows his body to take on that look of as many added years as he needs to make him comfortable and proper in that sort of society; he lets his body go on taking the look of age, according as he progresses, and by and by he will be bald and wrinkled outside, and wise and deep within."

"Babies the same?"

"Babies the same. Laws, what asses we used to be, on earth, about these things! We said we'd be always young in heaven. We didn't say *how* young— we didn't think of that, perhaps—that is, we didn't all think alike, anyway. When I was a boy of seven, I suppose I thought we'd all be twelve, in heaven; when I was twelve, I suppose I thought we'd all be eighteen or twenty in heaven; when I was forty, I begun to go back; I remember I hoped we'd all be about *thirty* years old in heaven. Neither a man nor a boy ever thinks the age he *has* is exactly the best one—he puts the right age a few years older or a few years younger than he is. Then he makes that ideal age the general age of the heavenly people. And he expects everybody *to stick* at that age—stand

26

stock-still—and expects them to enjoy it!—Now just think of the idea of standing still in heaven! Think of a heaven made up entirely of hoop-rolling, marble-playing cubs of seven years!—or of awkward, diffident, sentimental immaturities of nineteen!—or of vigorous people of thirty, healthy-minded, brimming with ambition, but chained hand and foot to that one age and its limitations like so many helpless galley-slaves! Think of the dull sameness of a society made up of people all of one age and one set of looks, habits, tastes and feelings. Think how superior to it earth would be, with its variety of types and faces and ages, and the enlivening attrition of the myriad interests that come into pleasant collision in such a variegated society."

"Look here," says I, "do you know what you're doing?"

"Well, what am I doing?"

"You are making heaven pretty comfortable in one way, but you are playing the mischief with it in another."

"How d'you mean?"

"Well," I says, "take a young mother that's lost her child, and—"

"Sh!" he says. "Look!"

It was a woman. Middle-aged, and had grizzled hair. She was walking slow, and her head was bent down, and her wings hanging limp and droopy; and she looked ever so tired, and was crying, poor thing! She passed along by, with her head down, that way, and the tears running down her face, and didn't see us. Then Sandy said, low and gentle, and full of pity:

"*She's* hunting for her child! No, *found* it, I reckon. Lord, how she's changed! But I recognized her in a minute, though it's twenty-seven years since I saw her. A young mother she was, about twenty two or four, or along there; and blooming and lovely and sweet? oh, just a flower! And all her heart and all her soul was wrapped up in her child, her little girl, two years old. And it died, and she went wild with grief, just wild! Well, the only comfort she had was that she'd see her child again, in heaven—'never more to part,' she said, and kept on saying it over and over, 'never more to part.' And the

27

words made her happy; yes, they did; they made her joyful, and when I was dying, twenty-seven years ago, she told me to find her child the first thing, and say she was coming—'soon, soon, *very* soon, she hoped and believed!'"

"Why, it's pitiful, Sandy."

He didn't say anything for a while, but sat looking at the ground, thinking. Then he says, kind of mournful:

"And now she's come!"

"Well? Go on."

"Stormfield, maybe she hasn't found the child, but *I* think she has. Looks so to me. I've seen cases before. You see, she's kept that child in her head just the same as it was when she jounced it in her arms a little chubby thing. But here it didn't elect to *stay* a child. No, it elected to grow up, which it did. And in these twenty-seven years it has learned all the deep scientific learning there is to learn, and is studying and studying and learning and learning more and more, all the time, and don't give a damn for anything *but* learning; just learning, and discussing gigantic problems with people like herself."

"Well?"

"Stormfield, don't you see? Her mother knows *cranberries*, and how to tend them, and pick them, and put them up, and market them; and not another blamed thing! Her and her daughter can't be any more company for each other *now* than mud turtle and bird o' paradise. Poor thing, she was looking for a baby to jounce; *I* think she's struck a disapp'intment."

"Sandy, what will they do—stay unhappy forever in heaven?"

"No, they'll come together and get adjusted by and by. But not this year, and not next. By and by."

CHAPTER II

I had been having considerable trouble with my wings. The day after I helped the choir I made a dash or two with them, but was not lucky. First off, I flew thirty yards, and then fouled an Irishman and brought him down—brought us both down, in fact. Next, I had a collision with a Bishop—and bowled him down, of course. We had some sharp words, and I felt pretty cheap, to come banging into a grave old person like that, with a million strangers looking on and smiling to themselves.

I saw I hadn't got the hang of the steering, and so couldn't rightly tell where I was going to bring up when I started. I went afoot the rest of the day, and let my wings hang. Early next morning I went to a private place to have some practice. I got up on a pretty high rock, and got a good start, and went swooping down, aiming for a bush a little over three hundred yards off; but I couldn't seem to calculate for the wind, which was about two points abaft my beam. I could see I was going considerable to looard of the bush, so I worked my starboard wing slow and went ahead strong on the port one, but it wouldn't answer; I could see I was going to broach to, so I slowed down on both, and lit. I went back to the rock and took another chance at it. I aimed two or three points to starboard of the bush—yes, more than that—enough so as to make it nearly a head-wind. I done well enough, but made pretty poor time. I could see, plain enough, that on a head-wind, wings was a mistake. I could see that a body could sail pretty close to the wind, but he couldn't go in the wind's eye. I could see that if I wanted to go a-visiting any distance from home, and the wind was ahead, I might have to wait days, maybe, for a change; and I could see, too, that these things could not be any use at all in a gale; if you tried to run before the wind, you would make a mess of it, for there isn't anyway to shorten sail—like reefing, you know—you have to take it *all* in—shut your feathers down flat to your sides. That would *land* you, of course. You could lay to, with your head to the wind—that is the best you could do, and right hard work you'd find it, too. If you tried any other game, you would founder, sure.

I judge it was about a couple of weeks or so after this that I dropped old Sandy McWilliams a note one day—it was a Tuesday—and asked him to come over and take his manna and quails with me next day; and the first thing he did when he stepped in was to twinkle his eye in a sly way, and say,—

"Well, Cap, what you done with your wings?"

I saw in a minute that there was some sarcasm done up in that rag somewheres, but I never let on. I only says,—

"Gone to the wash."

"Yes," he says, in a dry sort of way, "they mostly go to the wash—about this time—I've often noticed it. Fresh angels are powerful neat. When do you look for 'em back?"

"Day after to-morrow," says I.

He winked at me, and smiled.

Says I,—

"Sandy, out with it. Come—no secrets among friends. I notice you don't ever wear wings—and plenty others don't. I've been making an ass of myself—is that it?"

"That is about the size of it. But it is no harm. We all do it at first. It's perfectly natural. You see, on earth we jump to such foolish conclusions as to things up here. In the pictures we always saw the angels with wings on—and that was all right; but we jumped to the conclusion that that was their way of getting around—and that was all wrong. The wings ain't anything but a uniform, that's all. When they are in the field—so to speak,—they always wear them; you never see an angel going with a message anywhere without his wings, any more than you would see a military officer presiding at a court-martial without his uniform, or a postman delivering letters, or a policeman walking his beat, in plain clothes. But they ain't to *fly* with! The wings are for show, not for use. Old experienced angels are like officers of the regular army—they dress plain, when they are off duty. New angels are like the militia—never shed the uniform—always fluttering and floundering around in their wings, butting people down, flapping here, and there, and everywhere, always imagining they are attracting the admiring eye—well, they just think they are the very most important people in heaven. And when you see one of them come sailing around with one wing tipped up and t'other down, you make up your mind he is saying to himself: 'I wish Mary Ann in Arkansaw could see me now. I reckon she'd wish she hadn't shook me.' No, they're just for show, that's all—only just for show."

"I judge you've got it about right, Sandy," says I.

"Why, look at it yourself," says he. "*You* ain't built for wings—no man is. You know what a grist of years it took you to come here from the earth—and yet you were booming along faster than any cannon-ball could go. Suppose you had to fly that distance with your wings—wouldn't eternity have been over before you got here? Certainly. Well, angels have to go to the earth every day—millions of them—to appear in visions to dying children and good people, you know—it's the heft of their business. They appear with their wings, of course, because they are on official service, and because the dying persons wouldn't know they were angels if they hadn't wings— but do you reckon they fly with them? It stands to reason they don't. The wings would wear out before they got half-way; even the pin-feathers would be gone; the wing frames would be as bare as kite sticks before the paper is pasted on. The distances in heaven are billions of times greater; angels have to go all over heaven every day; could they do it with their wings alone? No, indeed; they wear the wings for style, but they travel any distance in an instant by *wishing*. The wishing-carpet of the Arabian Nights was a sensible idea—but our earthly idea of angels flying these awful distances with their clumsy wings was foolish.

"Our young saints, of both sexes, wear wings all the time—blazing red ones, and blue and green, and gold, and variegated, and rainbowed, and ring-streaked-and-striped ones—and nobody finds fault. It is suitable to their time of life. The things are beautiful, and they set the young people off. They are the most striking and lovely part of their outfit—a halo don't *begin*."

"Well," says I, "I've tucked mine away in the cupboard, and I allow to let them lay there till there's mud."

31

"Yes—or a reception."

"What's that?"

"Well, you can see one to-night if you want to. There's a barkeeper from Jersey City going to be received."

"Go on—tell me about it."

"This barkeeper got converted at a Moody and Sankey meeting, in New York, and started home on the ferry-boat, and there was a collision and he got drowned. He is of a class that think all heaven goes wild with joy when a particularly hard lot like him is saved; they think all heaven turns out hosannahing to welcome them; they think there isn't anything talked about in the realms of the blest but their case, for that day. This barkeeper thinks there hasn't been such another stir here in years, as his coming is going to raise.—And I've always noticed this peculiarity about a dead barkeeper—he not only expects all hands to turn out when he arrives, but he expects to be received with a torchlight procession."

"I reckon he is disappointed, then."

"No, he isn't. No man is allowed to be disappointed here. Whatever he wants, when he comes—that is, any reasonable and unsacrilegious thing—he can have. There's always a few millions or billions of young folks around who don't want any better entertainment than to fill up their lungs and swarm out with their torches and have a high time over a barkeeper. It tickles the barkeeper till he can't rest, it makes a charming lark for the young folks, it don't do anybody any harm, it don't cost a rap, and it keeps up the place's reputation for making all comers happy and content."

"Very good. I'll be on hand and see them land the barkeeper."

"It is manners to go in full dress. You want to wear your wings, you know, and your other things."

"Which ones?"

"Halo, and harp, and palm branch, and all that."

"Well," says I, "I reckon I ought to be ashamed of myself, but the fact is I left them laying around that day I resigned from the choir. I haven't got a rag to wear but this robe and the wings."

"That's all right. You'll find they've been raked up and saved for you. Send for them."

"I'll do it, Sandy. But what was it you was saying about unsacrilegious things, which people expect to get, and will be disappointed about?"

"Oh, there are a lot of such things that people expect and don't get. For instance, there's a Brooklyn preacher by the name of Talmage, who is laying up a considerable disappointment for himself. He says, every now and then in his sermons, that the first thing he does when he gets to heaven, will be to fling his arms around Abraham, Isaac and Jacob, and kiss them and weep on them. There's millions of people down there on earth that are promising themselves the same thing. As many as sixty thousand people arrive here every single day, that want to run straight to Abraham, Isaac and Jacob, and hug them and weep on them. Now mind you, sixty thousand a day is a pretty heavy contract for those old people. If they were a mind to allow it, they wouldn't ever have anything to do, year in and year out, but stand up and be hugged and wept on thirty-two hours in the twenty-four. They would be tired out and as wet as muskrats all the time. What would heaven be, to *them*? It would be a mighty good place to get out of—you know that, yourself. Those are kind and gentle old Jews, but they ain't any fonder of kissing the emotional highlights of Brooklyn than you be. You mark my words, Mr. T.'s endearments are going to be declined, with thanks. There are limits to the privileges of the elect, even in heaven. Why, if Adam was to show himself to every new comer that wants to call and gaze at him and strike him for his autograph, he would never have time to do anything else but just that. Talmage has said he is going to give Adam some of his attentions, as well as A., I. and J. But he will have to change his mind about that."

"Do you think Talmage will really come here?"

"Why, certainly, he will; but don't you be alarmed; he will run with his own kind, and there's plenty of them. That is the main charm of heaven—

there's all kinds here—which wouldn't be the case if you let the preachers tell it. Anybody can find the sort he prefers, here, and he just lets the others alone, and they let him alone. When the Deity builds a heaven, it is built right, and on a liberal plan."

Sandy sent home for his things, and I sent for mine, and about nine in the evening we begun to dress. Sandy says,—

"This is going to be a grand time for you, Stormy. Like as not some of the patriarchs will turn out."

"No, but will they?"

"Like as not. Of course they are pretty exclusive. They hardly ever show themselves to the common public. I believe they never turn out except for an eleventh-hour convert. They wouldn't do it then, only earthly tradition makes a grand show pretty necessary on that kind of an occasion."

"Do they an turn out, Sandy?"

"Who?—all the patriarchs? Oh, no—hardly ever more than a couple. You will be here fifty thousand years—maybe more—before you get a glimpse of all the patriarchs and prophets. Since I have been here, Job has been to the front once, and once Ham and Jeremiah both at the same time. But the finest thing that has happened in my day was a year or so ago; that was Charles Peace's reception—him they called 'the Bannercross Murderer'—an Englishman. There were four patriarchs and two prophets on the Grand Stand that time—there hasn't been anything like it since Captain Kidd came; Abel was there—the first time in twelve hundred years. A report got around that Adam was coming; well, of course, Abel was enough to bring a crowd, all by himself, but there is nobody that can draw like Adam. It was a false report, but it got around, anyway, as I say, and it will be a long day before I see the like of it again. The reception was in the English department, of course, which is eight hundred and eleven million miles from the New Jersey line. I went, along with a good many of my neighbors, and it was a sight to see, I can tell you. Flocks came from all the departments. I saw Esquimaux there, and Tartars, Negroes, Chinamen—people from everywhere. You see a mixture like that in the Grand Choir, the first day you land here, but you hardly ever see it again. There were billions of people; when they were singing or hosannahing, the noise was wonderful; and even when their tongues were still the drumming of the wings was nearly enough to burst your head, for all the sky was as thick as if it was snowing angels. Although Adam was not there, it was a great time anyway, because we had three archangels on the Grand Stand—it is a seldom thing that even one comes out."

"What did they look like, Sandy?"

"Well, they had shining faces, and shining robes, and wonderful rainbow wings, and they stood eighteen feet high, and wore swords, and held their heads up in a noble way, and looked like soldiers."

"Did they have halos?"

"No—anyway, not the hoop kind. The archangels and the upper-class patriarchs wear a finer thing than that. It is a round, solid, splendid glory of gold, that is blinding to look at. You have often seen a patriarch in a picture, on earth, with that thing on—you remember it?—he looks as if he had his head in a brass platter. That don't give you the right idea of it at all—it is much more shining and beautiful."

"Did you talk with those archangels and patriarchs, Sandy?"

"Who—I? Why, what can you be thinking about, Stormy? I ain't worthy to speak to such as they."

"Is Talmage?"

"Of course not. You have got the same mixed-up idea about these things that everybody has down there. I had it once, but I got over it. Down there they talk of the heavenly King—and that is right—but then they go right on speaking as if this was a republic and everybody was on a dead level with everybody else, and privileged to fling his arms around anybody he comes across, and be hail-fellow-well-met with all the elect, from the highest down. How tangled up and absurd that is! How are you going to have a republic under a king? How are you going to have a republic at all, where the head of the government is absolute, holds his place forever, and has no parliament, no council to meddle or make in his affairs, nobody voted for, nobody elected, nobody in the whole universe with a voice in the government, nobody asked to take a hand in its matters, and nobody *allowed* to do it? Fine republic, ain't it?"

"Well, yes—it *is* a little different from the idea I had—but I thought I might go around and get acquainted with the grandees, anyway—not exactly splice the main-brace with them, you know, but shake hands and pass the time of day."

"Could Tom, Dick and Harry call on the Cabinet of Russia and do that?—on Prince Gortschakoff, for instance?"

"I reckon not, Sandy."

"Well, this is Russia—only more so. There's not the shadow of a republic about it anywhere. There are ranks, here. There are viceroys, princes, governors, sub-governors, sub-sub-governors, and a hundred orders of nobility, grading along down from grand-ducal archangels, stage by stage, till the general level is struck, where there ain't any titles. Do you know what a prince of the blood is, on earth?"

"No."

"Well, a prince of the blood don't belong to the royal family exactly, and he don't belong to the mere nobility of the kingdom; he is lower than the one, and higher than t'other. That's about the position of the patriarchs and prophets here. There's some mighty high nobility here—people that you and I ain't worthy to polish sandals for—and *they* ain't worthy to polish sandals for the patriarchs and prophets. That gives you a kind of an idea of their rank, don't it? You begin to see how high up they are, don't you? just to get a two-minute glimpse of one of them is a thing for a body to remember and tell about for a thousand years. Why, Captain, just think of this: if Abraham was to set his foot down here by this door, there would be a railing set up around that foot-track right away, and a shelter put over it, and people would flock here from all over heaven, for hundreds and hundreds of years, to look

36

at it. Abraham is one of the parties that Mr. Talmage, of Brooklyn, is going to embrace, and kiss, and weep on, when he comes. He wants to lay in a good stock of tears, you know, or five to one he will go dry before he gets a chance to do it."

"Sandy," says I, "I had an idea that *I* was going to be equals with everybody here, too, but I will let that drop. It don't matter, and I am plenty happy enough anyway."

"Captain, you are happier than you would be, the other way. These old patriarchs and prophets have got ages the start of you; they know more in two minutes than you know in a year. Did you ever try to have a sociable improving-time discussing winds, and currents and variations of compass with an undertaker?"

"I get your idea, Sandy. He couldn't interest me. He would be an ignoramus in such things—he would bore me, and I would bore him."

"You have got it. You would bore the patriarchs when you talked, and when they talked they would shoot over your head. By and by you would say, 'Good morning, your Eminence, I will call again'—but you wouldn't. Did you ever ask the slush-boy to come up in the cabin and take dinner with you?"

"I get your drift again, Sandy. I wouldn't be used to such grand people as the patriarchs and prophets, and I would be sheepish and tongue-tied in their company, and mighty glad to get out of it. Sandy, which is the highest rank, patriarch or prophet?"

"Oh, the prophets hold over the patriarchs. The newest prophet, even, is of a sight more consequence than the oldest patriarch. Yes, sir, Adam himself has to walk behind Shakespeare."

"Was Shakespeare a prophet?"

"Of course he was; and so was Homer, and heaps more. But Shakespeare and the rest have to walk behind a common tailor from Tennessee, by the name of Billings; and behind a horse-doctor named Sakka, from Afghanistan.

Jeremiah, and Billings and Buddha walk together, side by side, right behind a crowd from planets not in our astronomy; next come a dozen or two from Jupiter and other worlds; next come Daniel, and Sakka and Confucius; next a lot from systems outside of ours; next come Ezekiel, and Mahomet, Zoroaster, and a knife-grinder from ancient Egypt; then there is a long string, and after them, away down toward the bottom, come Shakespeare and Homer, and a shoemaker named Marais, from the back settlements of France."

"Have they really rung in Mahomet and all those other heathens?"

"Yes—they all had their message, and they all get their reward. The man who don't get his reward on earth, needn't bother—he will get it here, sure."

"But why did they throw off on Shakespeare, that way, and put him away down there below those shoe-makers and horse-doctors and knife-grinders—a lot of people nobody ever heard of?"

"That is the heavenly justice of it—they warn't rewarded according to their deserts, on earth, but here they get their rightful rank. That tailor Billings, from Tennessee, wrote poetry that Homer and Shakespeare couldn't begin to come up to; but nobody would print it, nobody read it but his neighbors, an ignorant lot, and they laughed at it. Whenever the village had a drunken frolic and a dance, they would drag him in and crown him with cabbage leaves, and pretend to bow down to him; and one night when he was sick and nearly starved to death, they had him out and crowned him, and then they rode him on a rail about the village, and everybody followed along, beating tin pans and yelling. Well, he died before morning. He wasn't ever expecting to go to heaven, much less that there was going to be any fuss made over him, so I reckon he was a good deal surprised when the reception broke on him."

"Was you there, Sandy?"

"Bless you, no!"

"Why? Didn't you know it was going to come off?"

"Well, I judge I did. It was the talk of these realms—not for a day, like this barkeeper business, but for twenty years before the man died."

"Why the mischief didn't you go, then?"

"Now how you talk! The like of me go meddling around at the reception of a prophet? A mudsill like me trying to push in and help receive an awful grandee like Edward J. Billings? Why, I should have been laughed at for a billion miles around. I shouldn't ever heard the last of it."

"Well, who did go, then?"

"Mighty few people that you and I will ever get a chance to see, Captain. Not a solitary commoner ever has the luck to see a reception of a prophet, I can tell you. All the nobility, and all the patriarchs and prophets—every last one of them—and all the archangels, and all the princes and governors and viceroys, were there,—and *no* small fry—not a single one. And mind you, I'm not talking about only the grandees from *our* world, but the princes and patriarchs and so on from *all* the worlds that shine in our sky, and from billions more that belong in systems upon systems away outside of the one our sun is in. There were some prophets and patriarchs there that ours ain't a circumstance to, for rank and illustriousness and all that. Some were from Jupiter and other worlds in our own system, but the most celebrated were three poets, Saa, Bo and Soof, from great planets in three different and very remote systems. These three names are common and familiar in every nook and corner of heaven, clear from one end of it to the other—fully as well known as the eighty Supreme Archangels, in fact—where as our Moses, and Adam, and the rest, have not been heard of outside of our world's little corner of heaven, except by a few very learned men scattered here and there—and they always spell their names wrong, and get the performances of one mixed up with the doings of another, and they almost always locate them simply *in our solar system*, and think that is enough without going into little details such as naming the particular world they are from. It is like a learned Hindoo showing off how much he knows by saying Longfellow lives in the United States—as if he lived all over the United States, and as if the country was so small you couldn't throw a brick there without hitting him. Between you and me, it does gravel me, the cool way people from those monster worlds outside our system snub our little world, and even our system. Of course we think a good deal of Jupiter, because our world is only a potato to it, for size;

but then there are worlds in other systems that Jupiter isn't even a mustard-seed to—like the planet Goobra, for instance, which you couldn't squeeze inside the orbit of Halley's comet without straining the rivets. Tourists from Goobra (I mean parties that lived and died there—natives) come here, now and then, and inquire about our world, and when they find out it is so little that a streak of lightning can flash clear around it in the eighth of a second, they have to lean up against something to laugh. Then they screw a glass into their eye and go to examining us, as if we were a curious kind of foreign bug, or something of that sort. One of them asked me how long our day was; and when I told him it was twelve hours long, as a general thing, he asked me if people where I was from considered it worth while to get up and wash for such a day as that. That is the way with those Goobra people—they can't seem to let a chance go by to throw it in your face that their day is three hundred and twenty-two of our years long. This young snob was just of age—he was six or seven thousand of his days old—say two million of our years—and he had all the puppy airs that belong to that time of life—that turning-point when a person has got over being a boy and yet ain't quite a man exactly. If it had been anywhere else but in heaven, I would have given him a piece of my mind. Well, anyway, Billings had the grandest reception that has been seen in thousands of centuries, and I think it will have a good effect. His name will be carried pretty far, and it will make our system talked about, and maybe our world, too, and raise us in the respect of the general public of heaven. Why, look here—Shakespeare walked backwards before that tailor from Tennessee, and scattered flowers for him to walk on, and Homer stood behind his chair and waited on him at the banquet. Of course that didn't go for much *there*, amongst all those big foreigners from other systems, as they hadn't heard of Shakespeare or Homer either, but it would amount to considerable down there on our little earth if they could know about it. I wish there was something in that miserable spiritualism, so we could send them word. That Tennessee village would set up a monument to Billings, then, and his autograph would outsell Satan's. Well, they had grand times at that reception—a small-fry noble from Hoboken told me all about it—Sir Richard Duffer, Baronet."

"What, Sandy, a nobleman from Hoboken? How is that?"

"Easy enough. Duffer kept a sausage-shop and never saved a cent in his life because he used to give all his spare meat to the poor, in a quiet way. Not tramps,—no, the other sort—the sort that will starve before they will beg—honest square people out of work. Dick used to watch hungry-looking men and women and children, and track them home, and find out all about them from the neighbors, and then feed them and find them work. As nobody ever saw him give anything to anybody, he had the reputation of being mean; he died with it, too, and everybody said it was a good riddance; but the minute he landed here, they made him a baronet, and the very first words Dick the sausage-maker of Hoboken heard when he stepped upon the heavenly shore were, 'Welcome, Sir Richard Duffer!' It surprised him some, because he thought he had reasons to believe he was pointed for a warmer climate than this one."

All of a sudden the whole region fairly rocked under the crash of eleven hundred and one thunder blasts, all let off at once, and Sandy says,—

"There, that's for the barkeep."

I jumped up and says,—

"Then let's be moving along, Sandy; we don't want to miss any of this thing, you know."

"Keep your seat," he says; "he is only just telegraphed, that is all."

"How?"

"That blast only means that he has been sighted from the signal-station. He is off Sandy Hook. The committees will go down to meet him, now, and escort him in. There will be ceremonies and delays; they won't he coming up the Bay for a considerable time, yet. It is several billion miles away, anyway."

"*I* could have been a barkeeper and a hard lot just as well as not," says I, remembering the lonesome way I arrived, and how there wasn't any committee nor anything.

"I notice some regret in your voice," says Sandy, "and it is natural enough; but let bygones be bygones; you went according to your lights, and it is too late now to mend the thing."

"No, let it slide, Sandy, I don't mind. But you've got a Sandy Hook *here*, too, have you?"

"We've got everything here, just as it is below. All the States and Territories of the Union, and all the kingdoms of the earth and the islands of the sea are laid out here just as they are on the globe—all the same shape they are down there, and all graded to the relative size, only each State and realm and island is a good many billion times bigger here than it is below. There goes another blast."

"What is that one for?"

"That is only another fort answering the first one. They each fire eleven hundred and one thunder blasts at a single dash—it is the usual salute for an eleventh-hour guest; a hundred for each hour and an extra one for the guest's sex; if it was a woman we would know it by their leaving off the extra gun."

"How do we know there's eleven hundred and one, Sandy, when they all go off at once?—and yet we certainly do know."

"Our intellects are a good deal sharpened up, here, in some ways, and that is one of them. Numbers and sizes and distances are so great, here, that we have to be made so we can *feel* them—our old ways of counting and measuring and ciphering wouldn't ever give us an idea of them, but would only confuse us and oppress us and make our heads ache."

After some more talk about this, I says: "Sandy, I notice that I hardly ever see a white angel; where I run across one white angel, I strike as many as a hundred million copper-colored ones—people that can't speak English. How is that?"

"Well, you will find it the same in any State or Territory of the American corner of heaven you choose to go to. I have shot along, a whole week on a stretch, and gone millions and millions of miles, through perfect swarms

42

of angels, without ever seeing a single white one, or hearing a word I could understand. You see, America was occupied a billion years and more, by Injuns and Aztecs, and that sort of folks, before a white man ever set his foot in it. During the first three hundred years after Columbus's discovery, there wasn't ever more than one good lecture audience of white people, all put together, in America—I mean the whole thing, British Possessions and all; in the beginning of our century there were only 6,000,000 or 7,000,000— say seven; 12,000,000 or 14,000,000 in 1825; say 23,000,000 in 1850; 40,000,000 in 1875. Our death-rate has always been 20 in 1000 per annum. Well, 140,000 died the first year of the century; 280,000 the twenty-fifth year; 500,000 the fiftieth year; about a million the seventy-fifth year. Now I am going to be liberal about this thing, and consider that fifty million whites have died in America from the beginning up to to-day—make it sixty, if you want to; make it a hundred million—it's no difference about a few millions one way or t'other. Well, now, you can see, yourself, that when you come to spread a little dab of people like that over these hundreds of billions of miles of American territory here in heaven, it is like scattering a ten-cent box of homoeopathic pills over the Great Sahara and expecting to find them again. You can't expect us to amount to anything in heaven, and we *don't*—now that is the simple fact, and we have got to do the best we can with it. The learned men from other planets and other systems come here and hang around a while, when they are touring around the Kingdom, and then go back to their own section of heaven and write a book of travels, and they give America about five lines in it. And what do they say about us? They say this wilderness is populated with a scattering few hundred thousand billions of red angels, with now and then a curiously complected *diseased* one. You see, they think we whites and the occasional nigger are Injuns that have been bleached out or blackened by some leprous disease or other—for some peculiarly rascally*sin*, mind you. It is a mighty sour pill for us all, my friend—even the modestest of us, let alone the other kind, that think they are going to be received like a long-lost government bond, and hug Abraham into the bargain. I haven't asked you any of the particulars, Captain, but I judge it goes without saying—if my experience is worth anything—that there wasn't much of a hooraw made over you when you arrived—now was there?"

"Don't mention it, Sandy," says I, coloring up a little; "I wouldn't have had the family see it for any amount you are a mind to name. Change the subject, Sandy, change the subject."

"Well, do you think of settling in the California department of bliss?"

"I don't know. I wasn't calculating on doing anything really definite in that direction till the family come. I thought I would just look around, meantime, in a quiet way, and make up my mind. Besides, I know a good many dead people, and I was calculating to hunt them up and swap a little gossip with them about friends, and old times, and one thing or another, and ask them how they like it here, as far as they have got. I reckon my wife will want to camp in the California range, though, because most all her departed will be there, and she likes to be with folks she knows."

"Don't you let her. You see what the Jersey district of heaven is, for whites; well, the Californian district is a thousand times worse. It swarms with a mean kind of leather-headed mud-colored angels—and your nearest white neighbor is likely to be a million miles away. *What a man mostly misses, in heaven, is company*—company of his own sort and color and language. I have come near settling in the European part of heaven once or twice on that account."

"Well, why didn't you, Sandy?"

"Oh, various reasons. For one thing, although you *see* plenty of whites there, you can't understand any of them, hardly, and so you go about as hungry for talk as you do here. I like to look at a Russian or a German or an Italian—I even like to look at a Frenchman if I ever have the luck to catch him engaged in anything that ain't indelicate—but *looking* don't cure the hunger—what you want is talk."

"Well, there's England, Sandy—the English district of heaven."

"Yes, but it is not so very much better than this end of the heavenly domain. As long as you run across Englishmen born this side of three hundred years ago, you are all right; but the minute you get back of Elizabeth's time the language begins to fog up, and the further back you go the foggier it gets.

44

I had some talk with one Langland and a man by the name of Chaucer—old-time poets—but it was no use, I couldn't quite understand them, and they couldn't quite understand me. I have had letters from them since, but it is such broken English I can't make it out. Back of those men's time the English are just simply foreigners, nothing more, nothing less; they talk Danish, German, Norman French, and sometimes a mixture of all three; back of *them*, they talk Latin, and ancient British, Irish, and Gaelic; and then back of these come billions and billions of pure savages that talk a gibberish that Satan himself couldn't understand. The fact is, where you strike one man in the English settlements that you can understand, you wade through awful swarms that talk something you can't make head nor tail of. You see, every country on earth has been overlaid so often, in the course of a billion years, with different kinds of people and different sorts of languages, that this sort of mongrel business was bound to be the result in heaven."

"Sandy," says I, "did you see a good many of the great people history tells about?"

"Yes—plenty. I saw kings and all sorts of distinguished people."

"Do the kings rank just as they did below?"

"No; a body can't bring his rank up here with him. Divine right is a good-enough earthly romance, but it don't go, here. Kings drop down to the general level as soon as they reach the realms of grace. I knew Charles the Second very well—one of the most popular comedians in the English section—draws first rate. There are better, of course—people that were never heard of on earth—but Charles is making a very good reputation indeed, and is considered a rising man. Richard the Lion-hearted is in the prize-ring, and coming into considerable favor. Henry the Eighth is a tragedian, and the scenes where he kills people are done to the very life. Henry the Sixth keeps a religious-book stand."

"Did you ever see Napoleon, Sandy?"

"Often—sometimes in the Corsican range, sometimes in the French. He always hunts up a conspicuous place, and goes frowning around with his arms folded and his field-glass under his arm, looking as grand, gloomy and peculiar as his reputation calls for, and very much bothered because he don't stand as high, here, for a soldier, as he expected to."

"Why, who stands higher?"

"Oh, a *lot* of people *we* never heard of before—the shoemaker and horse-doctor and knife-grinder kind, you know—clodhoppers from goodness knows where that never handled a sword or fired a shot in their lives—but the soldiership was in them, though they never had a chance to show it. But here they take their right place, and Cæsar and Napoleon and Alexander have to take a back seat. The greatest military genius our world ever produced was a brick-layer from somewhere back of Boston—died during the Revolution— by the name of Absalom Jones. Wherever he goes, crowds flock to see him. You see, everybody knows that if he had had a chance he would have shown the world some generalship that would have made all generalship before look like child's play and 'prentice work. But he never got a chance; he tried heaps of times to enlist as a private, but he had lost both thumbs and a couple of front teeth, and the recruiting sergeant wouldn't pass him. However, as I say, everybody knows, now, what he *would* have been,—and so they flock by the million to get a glimpse of him whenever they hear he is going to be anywhere. Cæsar, and Hannibal, and Alexander, and Napoleon are all on his staff, and ever so many more great generals; but the public hardly care to look at *them* when *he* is around. Boom! There goes another salute. The barkeeper's off quarantine now."

Sandy and I put on our things. Then we made a wish, and in a second we were at the reception-place. We stood on the edge of the ocean of space, and looked out over the dimness, but couldn't make out anything. Close by us was the Grand Stand—tier on tier of dim thrones rising up toward the zenith. From each side of it spread away the tiers of seats for the general public. They spread away for leagues and leagues—you couldn't see the ends. They were empty and still, and hadn't a cheerful look, but looked dreary, like a theatre before anybody comes—gas turned down. Sandy says,—

"We'll sit down here and wait. We'll see the head of the procession come in sight away off yonder pretty soon, now."

Says I,—

"It's pretty lonesome, Sandy; I reckon there's a hitch somewheres. Nobody but just you and me—it ain't much of a display for the barkeeper."

"Don't you fret, it's all right. There'll be one more gun-fire—then you'll see."

In a little while we noticed a sort of a lightish flush, away off on the horizon.

"Head of the torchlight procession," says Sandy.

It spread, and got lighter and brighter: soon it had a strong glare like a locomotive headlight; it kept on getting brighter and brighter till it was like the sun peeping above the horizon-line at sea—the big red rays shot high up into the sky.

"Keep your eyes on the Grand Stand and the miles of seats—sharp!" says Sandy, "and listen for the gun-fire."

Just then it burst out, "Boom-boom-boom!" like a million thunderstorms in one, and made the whole heavens rock. Then there was a sudden and awful glare of light all about us, and in that very instant every one of the millions of seats was occupied, and as far as you could see, in both directions, was just a solid pack of people, and the place was all splendidly lit up! It was enough to take a body's breath away. Sandy says,—

"That is the way we do it here. No time fooled away; nobody straggling in after the curtain's up. Wishing is quicker work than travelling. A quarter of a second ago these folks were millions of miles from here. When they heard the last signal, all they had to do was to wish, and here they are."

The prodigious choir struck up,—

We long to hear thy voice,

To see thee face to face.

It was noble music, but the uneducated chipped in and spoilt it, just as the congregations used to do on earth.

The head of the procession began to pass, now, and it was a wonderful sight. It swept along, thick and solid, five hundred thousand angels abreast, and every angel carrying a torch and singing—the whirring thunder of the wings made a body's head ache. You could follow the line of the procession back, and slanting upward into the sky, far away in a glittering snaky rope, till it was only a faint streak in the distance. The rush went on and on, for a long time, and at last, sure enough, along comes the barkeeper, and then everybody rose, and a cheer went up that made the heavens shake, I tell you! He was all smiles, and had his halo tilted over one ear in a cocky way, and was the most satisfied-looking saint I ever saw. While he marched up the steps of the Grand Stand, the choir struck up,—

"The whole wide heaven groans,

And waits to hear that voice."

There were four gorgeous tents standing side by side in the place of honor, on a broad railed platform in the centre of the Grand Stand, with a shining guard of honor round about them. The tents had been shut up all this time. As the barkeeper climbed along up, bowing and smiling to everybody, and at last got to the platform, these tents were jerked up aloft all of a sudden, and we saw four noble thrones of gold, all caked with jewels, and in the two middle ones sat old white-whiskered men, and in the two others a couple of the most glorious and gaudy giants, with platter halos and beautiful armor. All the millions went down on their knees, and stared, and looked glad, and burst out into a joyful kind of murmurs. They said,—

"Two archangels!—that is splendid. Who can the others be?"

The archangels gave the barkeeper a stiff little military bow; the two old men rose; one of them said, "Moses and Esau welcome thee!" and then all the four vanished, and the thrones were empty.

The barkeeper looked a little disappointed, for he was calculating to hug those old people, I judge; but it was the gladdest and proudest multitude you ever saw—because they had seen Moses and Esau. Everybody was saying, "Did you see them?—I did—Esau's side face was to me, but I saw Moses full in the face, just as plain as I see you this minute!"

The procession took up the barkeeper and moved on with him again, and the crowd broke up and scattered. As we went along home, Sandy said it was a great success, and the barkeeper would have a right to be proud of it forever. And he said we were in luck, too; said we might attend receptions for forty thousand years to come, and not have a chance to see a brace of such grand moguls as Moses and Esau. We found afterwards that we had come near seeing another patriarch, and likewise a genuine prophet besides, but at the last moment they sent regrets. Sandy said there would be a monument put up there, where Moses and Esau had stood, with the date and circumstances, and all about the whole business, and travellers would come for thousands of years and gawk at it, and climb over it, and scribble their names on it.

<u>Footnotes:</u>

[9] The captain could not remember what this word was. He said it was in a foreign tongue.

About Author

Samuel Langhorne Clemens (November 30, 1835 – April 21, 1910), known by his pen name **Mark Twain**, was an American writer, humorist, entrepreneur, publisher, and lecturer. He was lauded as the "greatest humorist [the United States] has produced", and William Faulkner called him "the father of American literature". His novels include The Adventures of Tom Sawyer (1876) and its sequel, the Adventures of Huckleberry Finn (1884),the latter often called "The Great American Novel".

Twain was raised in Hannibal, Missouri, which later provided the setting for Tom Sawyer and Huckleberry Finn. He served an apprenticeship with a printer and then worked as a typesetter, contributing articles to the newspaper of his older brother Orion Clemens. He later became a riverboat pilot on the Mississippi River before heading west to join Orion in Nevada. He referred humorously to his lack of success at mining, turning to journalism for the Virginia City Territorial Enterprise. His humorous story, "The Celebrated Jumping Frog of Calaveras County", was published in 1865, based on a story that he heard at Angels Hotel in Angels Camp, California, where he had spent some time as a miner. The short story brought international attention and was even translated into French. His wit and satire, in prose and in speech, earned praise from critics and peers, and he was a friend to presidents, artists, industrialists, and European royalty.

Twain earned a great deal of money from his writings and lectures, but he invested in ventures that lost most of it—such as the Paige Compositor, a mechanical typesetter that failed because of its complexity and imprecision. He filed for bankruptcy in the wake of these financial setbacks, but he eventually overcame his financial troubles with the help of Henry Huttleston Rogers. He eventually paid all his creditors in full, even though his bankruptcy relieved him of having to do so. Twain was born shortly after an appearance of Halley's Comet, and he predicted that he would "go out with it" as well; he died the day after the comet returned.

Biography

Early life

Samuel Langhorne Clemens was born on November 30, 1835, in Florida, Missouri, the sixth of seven children born to Jane (née Lampton; 1803–1890), a native of Kentucky, and John Marshall Clemens (1798–1847), a native of Virginia. His parents met when his father moved to Missouri, and they were married in 1823. Twain was of Cornish, English, and Scots-Irish descent. Only three of his siblings survived childhood: Orion (1825–1897), Henry (1838–1858), and Pamela (1827–1904). His sister Margaret (1830–1839) died when Twain was three, and his brother Benjamin (1832–1842) died three years later. His brother Pleasant Hannibal (1828) died at three weeks of age.

When he was four, Twain's family moved to Hannibal, Missouri, a port town on the Mississippi River that inspired the fictional town of St. Petersburg in The Adventures of Tom Sawyer and the Adventures of Huckleberry Finn. Slavery was legal in Missouri at the time, and it became a theme in these writings. His father was an attorney and judge, who died of pneumonia in 1847, when Twain was 11. The next year, Twain left school after the fifth grade to become a printer's apprentice. In 1851, he began working as a typesetter, contributing articles and humorous sketches to the Hannibal Journal, a newspaper that Orion owned. When he was 18, he left Hannibal and worked as a printer in New York City, Philadelphia, St. Louis, and Cincinnati, joining the newly formed International Typographical Union, the printers trade union. He educated himself in public libraries in the evenings, finding wider information than at a conventional school.

Twain describes his boyhood in Life on the Mississippi, stating that "there was but one permanent ambition" among his comrades: to be a steamboatman.

> Pilot was the grandest position of all. The pilot, even in those days of trivial wages, had a princely salary – from a hundred and fifty to two hundred and fifty dollars a month, and no board to pay.

As Twain describes it, the pilot's prestige exceeded that of the captain. The pilot had to:

...get up a warm personal acquaintanceship with every old snag and one-limbed cottonwood and every obscure wood pile that ornaments the banks of this river for twelve hundred miles; and more than that, must... actually know where these things are in the dark

Steamboat pilot Horace E. Bixby took Twain on as a cub pilot to teach him the river between New Orleans and St. Louis for $500 (equivalent to $15,000 in 2019), payable out of Twain's first wages after graduating. Twain studied the Mississippi, learning its landmarks, how to navigate its currents effectively, and how to read the river and its constantly shifting channels, reefs, submerged snags, and rocks that would "tear the life out of the strongest vessel that ever floated". It was more than two years before he received his pilot's license. Piloting also gave him his pen name from "mark twain", the leadsman's cry for a measured river depth of two fathoms (12 feet), which was safe water for a steamboat.

As a young pilot, Clemens served on the steamer A. B. Chambers with Grant Marsh, who became famous for his exploits as a steamboat captain on the Missouri River. The two liked each other, and admired one another, and maintained a correspondence for many years after Clemens left the river.

While training, Samuel convinced his younger brother Henry to work with him, and even arranged a post of mud clerk for him on the steamboat Pennsylvania. On June 13, 1858, the steamboat's boiler exploded; Henry succumbed to his wounds on June 21. Twain claimed to have foreseen this death in a dream a month earlier,:275 which inspired his interest in parapsychology; he was an early member of the Society for Psychical Research Twain was guilt-stricken and held himself responsible for the rest of his life. He continued to work on the river and was a river pilot until the Civil War broke out in 1861, when traffic was curtailed along the Mississippi River. At the start of hostilities, he enlisted briefly in a local Confederate unit. He later wrote the sketch "The Private History of a Campaign That Failed", describing how he and his friends had been Confederate volunteers for two weeks before disbanding.

He then left for Nevada to work for his brother Orion, who was Secretary of the Nevada Territory. Twain describes the episode in his book Roughing It.

Travels

Orion became secretary to Nevada Territory governor James W. Nye in 1861, and Twain joined him when he moved west. The brothers traveled more than two weeks on a stagecoach across the Great Plains and the Rocky Mountains, visiting the Mormon community in Salt Lake City.

Twain's journey ended in the silver-mining town of Virginia City, Nevada, where he became a miner on the Comstock Lode. He failed as a miner and went to work at the Virginia City newspaper Territorial Enterprise, working under a friend, the writer Dan DeQuille. He first used his pen name here on February 3, 1863, when he wrote a humorous travel account entitled "Letter From Carson – re: Joe Goodman; party at Gov. Johnson's; music" and signed it "Mark Twain".

His experiences in the American West inspired Roughing It, written during 1870–71 and published in 1872. His experiences in Angels Camp (in Calaveras County, California) provided material for "The Celebrated Jumping Frog of Calaveras County" (1865).

Twain moved to San Francisco in 1864, still as a journalist, and met writers such as Bret Harte and Artemus Ward. He may have been romantically involved with the poet Ina Coolbrith.

His first success as a writer came when his humorous tall tale "The Celebrated Jumping Frog of Calaveras County" was published on November 18, 1865, in the New York weekly The Saturday Press, bringing him national attention. A year later, he traveled to the Sandwich Islands (present-day Hawaii) as a reporter for the Sacramento Union. His letters to the Union were popular and became the basis for his first lectures.

In 1867, a local newspaper funded his trip to the Mediterranean aboard the Quaker City, including a tour of Europe and the Middle East. He wrote a collection of travel letters which were later compiled as The Innocents Abroad (1869). It was on this trip that he met fellow passenger Charles Langdon, who showed him a picture of his sister Olivia. Twain later claimed to have fallen in love at first sight.

Upon returning to the United States, Twain was offered honorary membership in Yale University's secret society Scroll and Key in 1868. Its devotion to "fellowship, moral and literary self-improvement, and charity" suited him well.

Marriage and children

Twain and Olivia Langdon corresponded throughout 1868. She rejected his first marriage proposal, but they were married in Elmira, New York in February 1870, where he courted her and managed to overcome her father's initial reluctance. She came from a "wealthy but liberal family"; through her, he met abolitionists, "socialists, principled atheists and activists for women's rights and social equality", including Harriet Beecher Stowe (his next-door neighbor in Hartford, Connecticut), Frederick Douglass, and writer and utopian socialist William Dean Howells, who became a long-time friend. The couple lived in Buffalo, New York, from 1869 to 1871. He owned a stake in the Buffalo Express newspaper and worked as an editor and writer. While they were living in Buffalo, their son Langdon died of diphtheria at the age of 19 months. They had three daughters: Susy (1872–1896), Clara (1874–1962), and Jean (1880–1909).

Twain moved his family to Hartford, Connecticut, where he arranged the building of a home starting in 1873. In the 1870s and 1880s, the family summered at Quarry Farm in Elmira, the home of Olivia's sister, Susan Crane. In 1874, Susan had a study built apart from the main house so that Twain would have a quiet place in which to write. Also, he smoked cigars constantly, and Susan did not want him to do so in her house.

Twain wrote many of his classic novels during his 17 years in Hartford (1874–1891) and over 20 summers at Quarry Farm. They include The Adventures of Tom Sawyer (1876), The Prince and the Pauper (1881), Life on the Mississippi (1883), Adventures of Huckleberry Finn (1884), and A Connecticut Yankee in King Arthur's Court (1889).

The couple's marriage lasted 34 years until Olivia's death in 1904. All of the Clemens family are buried in Elmira's Woodlawn Cemetery.

Love of science and technology

Twain was fascinated with science and scientific inquiry. He developed a close and lasting friendship with Nikola Tesla, and the two spent much time together in Tesla's laboratory.

Twain patented three inventions, including an "Improvement in Adjustable and Detachable Straps for Garments" (to replace suspenders) and a history trivia game. Most commercially successful was a self-pasting scrapbook; a dried adhesive on the pages needed only to be moistened before use. Over 25,000 were sold.

Twain was an early proponent of fingerprinting as a forensic technique, featuring it in a tall tale in Life on the Mississippi (1883) and as a central plot element in the novel Pudd'nhead Wilson (1894).

Twain's novel A Connecticut Yankee in King Arthur's Court (1889) features a time traveler from the contemporary U.S., using his knowledge of science to introduce modern technology to Arthurian England. This type of historical manipulation became a trope of speculative fiction as alternate histories.

In 1909, Thomas Edison visited Twain at his home in Redding, Connecticut and filmed him. Part of the footage was used in The Prince and the Pauper (1909), a two-reel short film. It is the only known existing film footage of Twain.

Financial troubles

Twain made a substantial amount of money through his writing, but he lost a great deal through investments. He invested mostly in new inventions and technology, particularly the Paige typesetting machine. It was a beautifully engineered mechanical marvel that amazed viewers when it worked, but it was prone to breakdowns. Twain spent $300,000 (equal to $9,000,000 in inflation-adjusted terms) on it between 1880 and 1894, but before it could be perfected it was rendered obsolete by the Linotype. He lost the bulk of his book profits, as well as a substantial portion of his wife's inheritance.

Twain also lost money through his publishing house, Charles L. Webster and Company, which enjoyed initial success selling the memoirs of Ulysses S. Grant but failed soon afterward, losing money on a biography of Pope Leo XIII. Fewer than 200 copies were sold.

Twain and his family closed down their expensive Hartford home in response to the dwindling income and moved to Europe in June 1891. William M. Laffan of The New York Sun and the McClure Newspaper Syndicate offered him the publication of a series of six European letters. Twain, Olivia, and their daughter Susy were all faced with health problems, and they believed that it would be of benefit to visit European baths.:175 The family stayed mainly in France, Germany, and Italy until May 1895, with longer spells at Berlin (winter 1891/92), Florence (fall and winter 1892/93), and Paris (winters and springs 1893/94 and 1894/95). During that period, Twain returned four times to New York due to his enduring business troubles. He took "a cheap room" in September 1893 at $1.50 per day (equivalent to $43 in 2019) at The Players Club, which he had to keep until March 1894; meanwhile, he became "the Belle of New York," in the words of biographer Albert Bigelow Paine.

Twain's writings and lectures enabled him to recover financially, combined with the help of his friend, Henry Huttleston Rogers. He began a friendship with the financier in 1893, a principal of Standard Oil, that lasted the remainder of his life. Rogers first made him file for bankruptcy in April 1894, then had him transfer the copyrights on his written works to his wife to prevent creditors from gaining possession of them. Finally, Rogers took absolute charge of Twain's money until all his creditors were paid.

Twain accepted an offer from Robert Sparrow Smythe and embarked on a year-long, around the world lecture tour in July 1895 to pay off his creditors in full, although he was no longer under any legal obligation to do so. It was a long, arduous journey and he was sick much of the time, mostly from a cold and a carbuncle. The first part of the itinerary took him across northern America to British Columbia, Canada, until the second half of August. For the second part, he sailed across the Pacific Ocean. His scheduled lecture in Honolulu, Hawaii had to be canceled due to a cholera epidemic.[188] Twain went on to Fiji, Australia, New Zealand, Sri Lanka, India, Mauritius, and South Africa. His three months in India became the centerpiece of his 712-page book Following the Equator. In the second half of July 1896, he sailed back to England, completing his circumnavigation of the world begun 14 months before.

Twain and his family spent four more years in Europe, mainly in England and Austria (October 1897 to May 1899), with longer spells in London and Vienna. Clara had wished to study the piano under Theodor Leschetizky in Vienna.:192–211 However, Jean's health did not benefit from consulting with specialists in Vienna, the "City of Doctors". The family moved to London in spring 1899, following a lead by Poultney Bigelow who had a good experience being treated by Dr. Jonas Henrik Kellgren, a Swedish osteopathic practitioner in Belgravia. They were persuaded to spend the summer at Kellgren's sanatorium by the lake in the Swedish village of Sanna. Coming back in fall, they continued the treatment in London, until Twain was convinced by lengthy inquiries in America that similar osteopathic expertise was available there.

In mid-1900, he was the guest of newspaper proprietor Hugh Gilzean-Reid at Dollis Hill House, located on the north side of London. Twain wrote that he had "never seen any place that was so satisfactorily situated, with its noble trees and stretch of country, and everything that went to make life delightful, and all within a biscuit's throw of the metropolis of the world." He then returned to America in October 1900, having earned enough to pay off his debts. In winter 1900/01, he became his country's most prominent opponent of imperialism, raising the issue in his speeches, interviews, and writings. In January 1901, he began serving as vice-president of the Anti-Imperialist League of New York.

Speaking engagements

Twain was in great demand as a featured speaker, performing solo humorous talks similar to modern stand-up comedy. He gave paid talks to many men's clubs, including the Authors' Club, Beefsteak Club, Vagabonds, White Friars, and Monday Evening Club of Hartford.

In the late 1890s, he spoke to the Savage Club in London and was elected an honorary member. He was told that only three men had been so honored, including the Prince of Wales, and he replied: "Well, it must make the Prince feel mighty fine.":197 He visited Melbourne and Sydney in 1895 as part of a world lecture tour. In 1897, he spoke to the Concordia Press Club in Vienna as a special guest, following the diplomat Charlemagne Tower, Jr. He delivered the speech "Die Schrecken der Deutschen Sprache" ("The Horrors of the German Language")—in German—to the great amusement of the audience.:50 In 1901, he was invited to speak at Princeton University's Cliosophic Literary Society, where he was made an honorary member.

Canadian visits

In 1881, Twain was honored at a banquet in Montreal, Canada where he made reference to securing a copyright. In 1883, he paid a brief visit to Ottawa, and he visited Toronto twice in 1884 and 1885 on a reading tour with George Washington Cable, known as the "Twins of Genius" tour.

The reason for the Toronto visits was to secure Canadian and British copyrights for his upcoming book Adventures of Huckleberry Finn,to which he had alluded in his Montreal visit. The reason for the Ottawa visit had been to secure Canadian and British copyrights for Life on the Mississippi Publishers in Toronto had printed unauthorized editions of his books at the time, before an international copyright agreement was established in 1891. These were sold in the United States as well as in Canada, depriving him of royalties. He estimated that Belford Brothers' edition of The Adventures of Tom Sawyer alone had cost him ten thousand dollars (equivalent to $280,000 in 2019). He had unsuccessfully attempted to secure the rights for The Prince and the Pauper in 1881, in conjunction with his Montreal trip. Eventually, he received legal advice to register a copyright in Canada (for both Canada and Britain) prior to publishing in the United States, which would restrain the Canadian publishers from printing a version when the American edition was published. There was a requirement that a copyright be registered to a Canadian resident; he addressed this by his short visits to the country.

Later life and death

Twain lived in his later years at 14 West 10th Street in Manhattan. He passed through a period of deep depression which began in 1896 when his daughter Susy died of meningitis. Olivia's death in 1904 and Jean's on December 24, 1909, deepened his gloom. On May 20, 1909, his close friend Henry Rogers died suddenly. In April 1906, he heard that his friend Ina Coolbrith had lost nearly all that she owned in the 1906 San Francisco earthquake, and he volunteered a few autographed portrait photographs to be sold for her benefit. To further aid Coolbrith, George Wharton James visited Twain in New York and arranged for a new portrait session. He was resistant initially, but he eventually admitted that four of the resulting images were the finest ones ever taken of him. In September, Twain started publishing chapters from his autobiography in the North American Review. The same year, Charlotte Teller, a writer living with her grandmother at 3 Fifth Avenue, began an acquaintanceship with him which "lasted several years and may have included romantic intentions" on his part.

Twain formed a club in 1906 for girls whom he viewed as surrogate granddaughters called the Angel Fish and Aquarium Club. The dozen or so members ranged in age from 10 to 16. He exchanged letters with his "Angel Fish" girls and invited them to concerts and the theatre and to play games. Twain wrote in 1908 that the club was his "life's chief delight". In 1907, he met Dorothy Quick (aged 11) on a transatlantic crossing, beginning "a friendship that was to last until the very day of his death".

Oxford University awarded Twain an honorary doctorate in letters in 1907.

Twain was born two weeks after Halley's Comet's closest approach in 1835; he said in 1909:

I came in with Halley's Comet in 1835. It is coming again next year, and I expect to go out with it. It will be the greatest disappointment of my life if I don't go out with Halley's Comet. The Almighty has said, no doubt: "Now here are these two unaccountable freaks; they came in together, they must go out together".

Twain's prediction was accurate; he died of a heart attack on April 21, 1910, in Redding, Connecticut, one day after the comet's closest approach to Earth.

Upon hearing of Twain's death, President William Howard Taft said:

Mark Twain gave pleasure – real intellectual enjoyment – to millions, and his works will continue to give such pleasure to millions yet to come … His humor was American, but he was nearly as much appreciated by Englishmen and people of other countries as by his own countrymen. He has made an enduring part of American literature.

Twain's funeral was at the Brick Presbyterian Church on Fifth Avenue, New York. He is buried in his wife's family plot at Woodlawn Cemetery in Elmira, New York. The Langdon family plot is marked by a 12-foot monument (two fathoms, or "mark twain") placed there by his surviving daughter Clara. There is also a smaller headstone. He expressed a preference for cremation (for example, in Life on the Mississippi), but he acknowledged that his surviving family would have the last word.

Officials in Connecticut and New York estimated the value of Twain's estate at $471,000 ($13,000,000 today).

Writing

Overview

Twain began his career writing light, humorous verse, but he became a chronicler of the vanities, hypocrisies, and murderous acts of mankind. At mid-career, he combined rich humor, sturdy narrative, and social criticism in Huckleberry Finn. He was a master of rendering colloquial speech and helped to create and popularize a distinctive American literature built on American themes and language.

Many of his works have been suppressed at times for various reasons. The Adventures of Huckleberry Finn has been repeatedly restricted in American high schools, not least for its frequent use of the word "nigger", which was in common usage in the pre-Civil War period in which the novel was set.

A complete bibliography of Twain's works is nearly impossible to compile because of the vast number of pieces he wrote (often in obscure newspapers) and his use of several different pen names. Additionally, a large portion of his speeches and lectures have been lost or were not recorded; thus, the compilation of Twain's works is an ongoing process. Researchers rediscovered published material as recently as 1995 and 2015.

Early journalism and travelogues

Twain was writing for the Virginia City newspaper the Territorial Enterprise in 1863 when he met lawyer Tom Fitch, editor of the competing newspaper Virginia Daily Union and known as the "silver-tongued orator of the Pacific".:51 He credited Fitch with giving him his "first really profitable lesson" in writing. "When I first began to lecture, and in my earlier writings," Twain later commented, "my sole idea was to make comic capital out of everything I saw and heard." In 1866, he presented his lecture on the Sandwich Islands to a crowd in Washoe City, Nevada. Afterwards, Fitch told him:

> Clemens, your lecture was magnificent. It was eloquent, moving, sincere. Never in my entire life have I listened to such a magnificent piece of descriptive narration. But you committed one unpardonable sin – the unpardonable sin. It is a sin you must never commit again. You closed a most eloquent description, by which you had keyed your audience up to a pitch of the intensest interest, with a piece of atrocious anti-climax which nullified all the really fine effect you had produced.

It was in these days that Twain became a writer of the Sagebrush School; he was known later as its most famous member. His first important work was "The Celebrated Jumping Frog of Calaveras County," published in the New York Saturday Press on November 18, 1865. After a burst of popularity, the Sacramento Union commissioned him to write letters about his travel experiences. The first journey that he took for this job was to ride the steamer Ajax on its maiden voyage to the Sandwich Islands (Hawaii). All the while, he was writing letters to the newspaper that were meant for publishing, chronicling his experiences with humor. These letters proved to be the genesis to his work with the San Francisco Alta California newspaper, which designated him a traveling correspondent for a trip from San Francisco to New York City via the Panama isthmus.

On June 8, 1867, he set sail on the pleasure cruiser Quaker City for five months, and this trip resulted in The Innocents Abroad or The New Pilgrims' Progress. In 1872, he published his second piece of travel literature, Roughing It, as an account of his journey from Missouri to Nevada, his subsequent life in the American West, and his visit to Hawaii. The book lampoons American and Western society in the same way that Innocents critiqued the various countries of Europe and the Middle East. His next work was The Gilded Age: A Tale of Today, his first attempt at writing a novel. The book, written with his neighbor Charles Dudley Warner, is also his only collaboration.

Twain's next work drew on his experiences on the Mississippi River. Old Times on the Mississippi was a series of sketches published in the Atlantic Monthly in 1875 featuring his disillusionment with Romanticism. Old Times eventually became the starting point for Life on the Mississippi.

Tom Sawyer and Huckleberry Finn

Twain's next major publication was The Adventures of Tom Sawyer, which draws on his youth in Hannibal. Tom Sawyer was modeled on Twain as a child, with traces of schoolmates John Briggs and Will Bowen. The book also introduces Huckleberry Finn in a supporting role, based on Twain's boyhood friend Tom Blankenship.

The Prince and the Pauper was not as well received, despite a storyline that is common in film and literature today. The book tells the story of two boys born on the same day who are physically identical, acting as a social commentary as the prince and pauper switch places. Twain had started Adventures of Huckleberry Finn (which he consistently had problems completing) and had completed his travel book A Tramp Abroad, which describes his travels through central and southern Europe.

Twain's next major published work was the Adventures of Huckleberry Finn, which confirmed him as a noteworthy American writer. Some have called it the first Great American Novel, and the book has become required reading in many schools throughout the United States. Huckleberry Finn was an offshoot from Tom Sawyer and had a more serious tone than its predecessor. Four hundred manuscript pages were written in mid-1876, right after the publication of Tom Sawyer. The last fifth of Huckleberry Finn is subject to much controversy. Some say that Twain experienced a "failure of nerve," as critic Leo Marx puts it. Ernest Hemingway once said of Huckleberry Finn:

> If you read it, you must stop where the Nigger Jim is stolen from the boys. That is the real end. The rest is just cheating.

Hemingway also wrote in the same essay:

> All modern American literature comes from one book by Mark Twain called Huckleberry Finn.

Near the completion of Huckleberry Finn, Twain wrote Life on the Mississippi, which is said to have heavily influenced the novel. The travel work recounts Twain's memories and new experiences after a 22-year absence from the Mississippi River. In it, he also explains that "Mark Twain" was the call made when the boat was in safe water, indicating a depth of two fathoms (12 feet or 3.7 metres).

Later writing

Twain produced President Ulysses S. Grant's Memoirs through his fledgling publishing house, Charles L. Webster & Company, which he co-owned with Charles L. Webster, his nephew by marriage.

At this time he also wrote "The Private History of a Campaign That Failed" for The Century Magazine. This piece detailed his two-week stint in a Confederate militia during the Civil War. He next focused on A Connecticut Yankee in King Arthur's Court, written with the same historical fiction style as The Prince and the Pauper. A Connecticut Yankee showed the absurdities of political and social norms by setting them in the court of King Arthur. The book was started in December 1885, then shelved a few months later until the summer of 1887, and eventually finished in the spring of 1889.

His next large-scale work was Pudd'nhead Wilson, which he wrote rapidly, as he was desperately trying to stave off bankruptcy. From November 12 to December 14, 1893, Twain wrote 60,000 words for the novel. Critics[who?] have pointed to this rushed completion as the cause of the novel's rough organization and constant disruption of the plot. This novel also contains the tale of two boys born on the same day who switch positions in life, like The Prince and the Pauper. It was first published serially in Century Magazine and, when it was finally published in book form, Pudd'nhead Wilson appeared as the main title; however, the "subtitles" make the entire title read: The Tragedy of Pudd'nhead Wilson and the Comedy of The Extraordinary Twins.

Twain's next venture was a work of straight fiction that he called Personal Recollections of Joan of Arc and dedicated to his wife. He had long said[where?] that this was the work that he was most proud of, despite the criticism that he received for it. The book had been a dream of his since childhood, and he claimed that he had found a manuscript detailing the life of Joan of Arc when he was an adolescent. This was another piece that he was convinced would save his publishing company. His financial adviser Henry Huttleston Rogers quashed that idea and got Twain out of that business altogether, but the book was published nonetheless.

To pay the bills and keep his business projects afloat, Twain had begun to write articles and commentary furiously, with diminishing returns, but it was not enough. He filed for bankruptcy in 1894. During this time of dire financial straits, he published several literary reviews in newspapers to help make ends meet. He famously derided James Fenimore Cooper in his article detailing Cooper's "Literary Offenses". He became an extremely outspoken critic of other authors and other critics; he suggested that, before praising Cooper's work, Thomas Lounsbury, Brander Matthews, and Wilkie Collins "ought to have read some of it".

George Eliot, Jane Austen, and Robert Louis Stevenson also fell under Twain's attack during this time period, beginning around 1890 and continuing until his death. He outlines what he considers to be "quality writing" in several letters and essays, in addition to providing a source for the "tooth and claw" style of literary criticism. He places emphasis on concision, utility of word choice, and realism; he complains, for example, that Cooper's Deerslayer purports to be realistic but has several shortcomings. Ironically, several of his own works were later criticized for lack of continuity (Adventures of Huckleberry Finn) and organization (Pudd'nhead Wilson).

Twain's wife died in 1904 while the couple were staying at the Villa di Quarto in Florence. After some time had passed he published some works that his wife, his de facto editor and censor throughout her married life, had looked down upon. The Mysterious Stranger is perhaps the best known, depicting various visits of Satan to earth. This particular work was not published in Twain's lifetime. His manuscripts included three versions, written between 1897 and 1905: the so-called Hannibal, Eseldorf, and Print Shop versions. The resulting confusion led to extensive publication of a jumbled version, and only recently have the original versions become available as Twain wrote them.

Twain's last work was his autobiography, which he dictated and thought would be most entertaining if he went off on whims and tangents in non-chronological order. Some archivists and compilers have rearranged the biography into a more conventional form, thereby eliminating some of Twain's humor and the flow of the book. The first volume of the autobiography, over 736 pages, was published by the University of California in November 2010, 100 years after his death, as Twain wished. It soon became an unexpected best-seller, making Twain one of a very few authors publishing new best-selling volumes in the 19th, 20th, and 21st centuries.

Censorship

Twain's works have been subjected to censorship efforts. According to Stuart (2013), "Leading these banning campaigns, generally, were religious organizations or individuals in positions of influence – not so much working librarians, who had been instilled with that American "library spirit" which honored intellectual freedom (within bounds of course)". In 1905, the Brooklyn Public Library banned both The Adventures of Huckleberry Finn and The Adventures of Tom Sawyer from the children's department because of their language.

Views

Twain's views became more radical as he grew older. In a letter to friend and fellow writer William Dean Howells in 1887 he acknowledged that his views had changed and developed over his lifetime, referring to one of his favorite works:

When I finished Carlyle's French Revolution in 1871, I was a Girondin; every time I have read it since, I have read it differently – being influenced and changed, little by little, by life and environment ... and now I lay the book down once more, and recognize that I am a Sansculotte! And not a pale, characterless Sansculotte, but a Marat.

Anti-imperialist

Before 1899, Twain was an ardent imperialist. In the late 1860s and early 1870s, he spoke out strongly in favor of American interests in the Hawaiian Islands. He said the war with Spain in 1898 was "the worthiest" war ever fought. In 1899, however, he reversed course. In the New York Herald, October 16, 1900, Twain describes his transformation and political awakening, in the context of the Philippine–American War, to anti-imperialism:

I wanted the American eagle to go screaming into the Pacific ... Why not spread its wings over the Philippines, I asked myself? ... I said to myself, Here are a people who have suffered for three centuries. We can make them as free as ourselves, give them a government and country of their own, put a miniature of the American Constitution afloat in the Pacific, start a brand new republic to take its place among the free nations of the world. It seemed to me a great task to which we had addressed ourselves.

But I have thought some more, since then, and I have read carefully the treaty of Paris [which ended the Spanish–American War], and I have seen that we do not intend to free, but to subjugate the people of the Philippines. We have gone there to conquer, not to redeem.

It should, it seems to me, be our pleasure and duty to make those people free, and let them deal with their own domestic questions in their own way. And so I am an anti-imperialist. I am opposed to having the eagle put its talons on any other land.

During the Boxer rebellion, Twain said that "the Boxer is a patriot. He loves his country better than he does the countries of other people. I wish him success."

From 1901, soon after his return from Europe, until his death in 1910, Twain was vice-president of the American Anti-Imperialist League, which opposed the annexation of the Philippines by the United States and had "tens of thousands of members". He wrote many political pamphlets for the organization. The Incident in the Philippines, posthumously published in 1924, was in response to the Moro Crater Massacre, in which six hundred Moros were killed. Many of his neglected and previously uncollected writings on anti-imperialism appeared for the first time in book form in 1992.

Twain was critical of imperialism in other countries as well. In Following the Equator, Twain expresses "hatred and condemnation of imperialism of all stripes". He was highly critical of European imperialists, such as Cecil Rhodes, who greatly expanded the British Empire, and Leopold II, King of the Belgians. King Leopold's Soliloquy is a stinging political satire about his private colony, the Congo Free State. Reports of outrageous exploitation and grotesque abuses led to widespread international protest in the early 1900s, arguably the first large-scale human rights movement. In the soliloquy, the King argues that bringing Christianity to the country outweighs a little starvation. Leopold's rubber gatherers were tortured, maimed and slaughtered until the movement forced Brussels to call a halt.

During the Philippine–American War, Twain wrote a short pacifist story titled The War Prayer, which makes the point that humanism and Christianity's preaching of love are incompatible with the conduct of war. It was submitted to Harper's Bazaar for publication, but on March 22, 1905, the magazine rejected the story as "not quite suited to a woman's magazine". Eight days later, Twain wrote to his friend Daniel Carter Beard, to whom he had read the story, "I don't think the prayer will be published in my time. None but the dead are permitted to tell the truth." Because he had an exclusive contract with Harper & Brothers, Twain could not publish The War Prayer elsewhere; it remained unpublished until 1923. It was republished as campaigning material by Vietnam War protesters.

Twain acknowledged that he had originally sympathized with the more moderate Girondins of the French Revolution and then shifted his sympathies to the more radical Sansculottes, indeed identifying himself as "a Marat" and writing that the Reign of Terror paled in comparison to the older terrors that preceded it. Twain supported the revolutionaries in Russia against the reformists, arguing that the Tsar must be got rid of by violent means, because peaceful ones would not work. He summed up his views of revolutions in the following statement:

> I am said to be a revolutionist in my sympathies, by birth, by breeding and by principle. I am always on the side of the revolutionists, because there never was a revolution unless there were some oppressive and intolerable conditions against which to revolute.

Civil rights

Twain was an adamant supporter of the abolition of slavery and the emancipation of slaves, even going so far as to say, "Lincoln's Proclamation ... not only set the black slaves free, but set the white man free also". He argued that non-whites did not receive justice in the United States, once saying, "I have seen Chinamen abused and maltreated in all the mean, cowardly ways possible to the invention of a degraded nature ... but I never saw a Chinaman righted in a court of justice for wrongs thus done to him". He paid for at least one black person to attend Yale Law School and for another black person to attend a southern university to become a minister.

Twain's sympathetic views on race were not reflected in his early writings on American Indians. Of them, Twain wrote in 1870:

> His heart is a cesspool of falsehood, of treachery, and of low and devilish instincts. With him, gratitude is an unknown emotion; and when one does him a kindness, it is safest to keep the face toward him, lest the reward be an arrow in the back. To accept of a favor from him is

to assume a debt which you can never repay to his satisfaction, though you bankrupt yourself trying. The scum of the earth!

As counterpoint, Twain's essay on "The Literary Offenses of Fenimore Cooper" offers a much kinder view of Indians. "No, other Indians would have noticed these things, but Cooper's Indians never notice anything. Cooper thinks they are marvelous creatures for noticing, but he was almost always in error about his Indians. There was seldom a sane one among them." In his later travelogue Following the Equator (1897), Twain observes that in colonized lands all over the world, "savages" have always been wronged by "whites" in the most merciless ways, such as "robbery, humiliation, and slow, slow murder, through poverty and the white man's whiskey"; his conclusion is that "there are many humorous things in this world; among them the white man's notion that he is less savage than the other savages". In an expression that captures his East Indian experiences, he wrote, "So far as I am able to judge nothing has been left undone, either by man or Nature, to make India the most extraordinary country that the sun visits on his rounds. Where every prospect pleases, and only man is vile."

Twain was also a staunch supporter of women's rights and an active campaigner for women's suffrage. His "Votes for Women" speech, in which he pressed for the granting of voting rights to women, is considered one of the most famous in history.

Helen Keller benefited from Twain's support as she pursued her college education and publishing despite her disabilities and financial limitations. The two were friends for roughly 16 years.

Through Twain's efforts, the Connecticut legislature voted a pension for Prudence Crandall, since 1995 Connecticut's official heroine, for her efforts towards the education of African-American young ladies in Connecticut. Twain also offered to purchase for her use her former house in Canterbury, home of the Canterbury Female Boarding School, but she declined.

Labor

Twain wrote glowingly about unions in the river boating industry in

Life on the Mississippi, which was read in union halls decades later. He supported the labor movement, especially one of the most important unions, the Knights of Labor. In a speech to them, he said:

> Who are the oppressors? The few: the King, the capitalist, and a handful of other overseers and superintendents. Who are the oppressed? The many: the nations of the earth; the valuable personages; the workers; they that make the bread that the soft-handed and idle eat.

Religion

Twain was a Presbyterian. He was critical of organized religion and certain elements of Christianity through his later life. He wrote, for example, "Faith is believing what you know ain't so", and "If Christ were here now there is one thing he would not be – a Christian". With anti-Catholic sentiment rampant in 19th century America, Twain noted he was "educated to enmity toward everything that is Catholic". As an adult, he engaged in religious discussions and attended services, his theology developing as he wrestled with the deaths of loved ones and with his own mortality.

Twain generally avoided publishing his most controversial opinions on religion in his lifetime, and they are known from essays and stories that were published later. In the essay Three Statements of the Eighties in the 1880s, Twain stated that he believed in an almighty God, but not in any messages, revelations, holy scriptures such as the Bible, Providence, or retribution in the afterlife. He did state that "the goodness, the justice, and the mercy of God are manifested in His works", but also that "the universe is governed by strict and immutable laws", which determine "small matters", such as who dies in a pestilence. At other times, he wrote or spoke in ways that contradicted a strict deist view, for example, plainly professing a belief in Providence. In some later writings in the 1890s, he was less optimistic about the goodness of God, observing that "if our Maker is all-powerful for good or evil, He is not in His right mind". At other times, he conjectured sardonically that perhaps God had created the world with all its tortures for some purpose of His own, but was otherwise indifferent to humanity, which was too petty and insignificant to deserve His attention anyway.

In 1901, Twain criticized the actions of the missionary Dr. William Scott Ament (1851–1909) because Ament and other missionaries had collected indemnities from Chinese subjects in the aftermath of the Boxer Uprising of 1900. Twain's response to hearing of Ament's methods was published in the North American Review in February 1901: To the Person Sitting in Darkness, and deals with examples of imperialism in China, South Africa, and with the U.S. occupation of the Philippines. A subsequent article, "To My Missionary Critics" published in The North American Review in April 1901, unapologetically continues his attack, but with the focus shifted from Ament to his missionary superiors, the American Board of Commissioners for Foreign Missions.

After his death, Twain's family suppressed some of his work that was especially irreverent toward conventional religion, including Letters from the Earth, which was not published until his daughter Clara reversed her position in 1962 in response to Soviet propaganda about the withholding. The anti-religious The Mysterious Stranger was published in 1916. Little Bessie, a story ridiculing Christianity, was first published in the 1972 collection Mark Twain's Fables of Man.

He raised money to build a Presbyterian Church in Nevada in 1864.

Twain created a reverent portrayal of Joan of Arc, a subject over which he had obsessed for forty years, studied for a dozen years and spent two years writing about. In 1900 and again in 1908 he stated, "I like Joan of Arc best of all my books, it is the best".

Those who knew Twain well late in life recount that he dwelt on the subject of the afterlife, his daughter Clara saying: "Sometimes he believed death ended everything, but most of the time he felt sure of a life beyond."

Twain's frankest views on religion appeared in his final work Autobiography of Mark Twain, the publication of which started in November 2010, 100 years after his death. In it, he said:

> There is one notable thing about our Christianity: bad, bloody, merciless, money-grabbing, and predatory as it is – in our country

particularly and in all other Christian countries in a somewhat modified degree – it is still a hundred times better than the Christianity of the Bible, with its prodigious crime – the invention of Hell. Measured by our Christianity of to-day, bad as it is, hypocritical as it is, empty and hollow as it is, neither the Deity nor his Son is a Christian, nor qualified for that moderately high place. Ours is a terrible religion. The fleets of the world could swim in spacious comfort in the innocent blood it has spilled.

Twain was a Freemason. He belonged to Polar Star Lodge No. 79 A.F.&A.M., based in St. Louis. He was initiated an Entered Apprentice on May 22, 1861, passed to the degree of Fellow Craft on June 12, and raised to the degree of Master Mason on July 10.

Twain visited Salt Lake City for two days and met there members of The Church of Jesus Christ of Latter-day Saints. They also gave him a Book of Mormon. He later wrote in Roughing It about that book:

> The book seems to be merely a prosy detail of imaginary history, with the Old Testament for a model; followed by a tedious plagiarism of the New Testament.

Vivisection

Twain was opposed to the vivisection practices of his day. His objection was not on a scientific basis but rather an ethical one. He specifically cited the pain caused to the animal as his basis of his opposition:

> I am not interested to know whether Vivisection produces results that are profitable to the human race or doesn't. … The pains which it inflicts upon unconsenting animals is the basis of my enmity towards it, and it is to me sufficient justification of the enmity without looking further.

Pen names

Twain used different pen names before deciding on "Mark Twain". He signed humorous and imaginative sketches as "Josh" until 1863. Additionally, he used the pen name "Thomas Jefferson Snodgrass" for a series of humorous letters.

He maintained that his primary pen name came from his years working on Mississippi riverboats, where two fathoms, a depth indicating water safe for the passage of boat, was a measure on the sounding line. Twain is an archaic term for "two", as in "The veil of the temple was rent in twain." The riverboatman's cry was "mark twain" or, more fully, "by the mark twain", meaning "according to the mark [on the line], [the depth is] two [fathoms]", that is, "The water is 12 feet (3.7 m) deep and it is safe to pass."

Twain said that his famous pen name was not entirely his invention. In Life on the Mississippi, he wrote:

> Captain Isaiah Sellers was not of literary turn or capacity, but he used to jot down brief paragraphs of plain practical information about the river, and sign them "MARK TWAIN", and give them to the New Orleans Picayune. They related to the stage and condition of the river, and were accurate and valuable; ... At the time that the telegraph brought the news of his death, I was on the Pacific coast. I was a fresh new journalist, and needed a nom de guerre; so I confiscated the ancient mariner's discarded one, and have done my best to make it remain what it was in his hands – a sign and symbol and warrant that whatever is found in its company may be gambled on as being the petrified truth; how I have succeeded, it would not be modest in me to say.

Twain's story about his pen name has been questioned by some with the suggestion that "mark twain" refers to a running bar tab that Twain would regularly incur while drinking at John Piper's saloon in Virginia City, Nevada. Samuel Clemens himself responded to this suggestion by saying, "Mark Twain was the nom de plume of one Captain Isaiah Sellers, who used to write river news over it for the New Orleans Picayune. He died in 1869 and as he could no longer need that signature, I laid violent hands upon it without asking permission of the proprietor's remains. That is the history of the nom de plume I bear."

In his autobiography, Twain writes further of Captain Sellers' use of "Mark Twain":

> I was a cub pilot on the Mississippi River then, and one day

I wrote a rude and crude satire which was leveled at Captain Isaiah Sellers, the oldest steamboat pilot on the Mississippi River, and the most respected, esteemed, and revered. For many years he had occasionally written brief paragraphs concerning the river and the changes which it had undergone under his observation during fifty years, and had signed these paragraphs "Mark Twain" and published them in the St. Louis and New Orleans journals. In my satire I made rude game of his reminiscences. It was a shabby poor performance, but I didn't know it, and the pilots didn't know it. The pilots thought it was brilliant. They were jealous of Sellers, because when the gray-heads among them pleased their vanity by detailing in the hearing of the younger craftsmen marvels which they had seen in the long ago on the river, Sellers was always likely to step in at the psychological moment and snuff them out with wonders of his own which made their small marvels look pale and sick. However, I have told all about this in "Old Times on the Mississippi." The pilots handed my extravagant satire to a river reporter, and it was published in the New Orleans True Delta. That poor old Captain Sellers was deeply wounded. He had never been held up to ridicule before; he was sensitive, and he never got over the hurt which I had wantonly and stupidly inflicted upon his dignity. I was proud of my performance for a while, and considered it quite wonderful, but I have changed my opinion of it long ago. Sellers never published another paragraph nor ever used his nom de guerre again.

Legacy and depictions

Trademark white suit

While Twain is often depicted wearing a white suit, modern representations suggesting that he wore them throughout his life are unfounded. Evidence suggests that Twain began wearing white suits on the lecture circuit, after the death of his wife Olivia ("Livy") in 1904. However, there is also evidence showing him wearing a white suit before 1904. In 1882, he sent a photograph of himself in a white suit to 18-year-old Edward W. Bok, later publisher of the Ladies Home Journal, with a handwritten dated note. The white suit did eventually become his trademark, as illustrated in anecdotes about this eccentricity (such as the time he wore a white summer suit to a Congressional hearing during the winter). McMasters' The Mark Twain Encyclopedia states that Twain did not wear a white suit in his last three years, except at one banquet speech.

In his autobiography, Twain writes of his early experiments with wearing white out-of-season:

> Next after fine colors, I like plain white. One of my sorrows, when the summer ends, is that I must put off my cheery and comfortable white clothes and enter for the winter into the depressing captivity of the shapeless and degrading black ones. It is mid-October now, and the weather is growing cold up here in the New Hampshire hills, but it will not succeed in freezing me out of these white garments, for here the neighbors are few, and it is only of crowds that I am afraid. (Source wikipedia)

NOTABLE WORKS

NOVELS

The Gilded Age: A Tale of Today (1873)

The Prince and the Pauper (1881)

A Connecticut Yankee in King Arthur's Court (1889)

The American Claimant (1892)

Pudd'nhead Wilson (1894)

Personal Recollections of Joan of Arc (1896)

A Horse's Tale (1907)

The Mysterious Stranger (1916, posthumous)

TOM SAWYER AND HUCKLEBERRY FINN

The Adventures of Tom Sawyer (1876)

Adventures of Huckleberry Finn (1884)

Tom Sawyer Abroad (1894)

Tom Sawyer, Detective (1896)

"Schoolhouse Hill" (6 chapters) in The Mysterious Stranger (c.1898, unfinished)

"Huck Finn and Tom Sawyer among the Indians" (c. 1884, 9 chapters, unfinished)

"Huck Finn" (1903, unfinished)

"Tom Sawyer's Conspiracy" (10 chapters, unfinished)

"Tom Sawyer's Gang Plans a Naval Battle" (unfinished)

ADAM AND EVE

"Extracts from Adam's Diary", illustrated by Frederick Strothmann (1904)

"Eve's Diary", illustrated by Lester Ralph (1906)

"The Private Life of Adam and Eve: Being Extracts from Their Diaries, Translated from the Original Mss." – posthumous issue of the 1904 and 1906 works bound as one, as Twain had requested in a recently discovered letter

SHORT STORIES

"The Celebrated Jumping Frog of Calaveras County" (1865)

"Advice to Little Girls" (1865)

"General Washington's Negro Body-Servant" (1868)

"Cannibalism in the Cars" (1868)

"My Late Senatorial Secretaryship" (1868)

"A Ghost Story" (1870)

"A True Story, Repeated Word for Word As I Heard It" (1874)

"Some Learned Fables for Good Old Boys and Girls" (1875)

"The Story Of The Bad Little Boy" (1875)

"The Story Of The Good Little Boy" (1875)

"A Literary Nightmare" (1876)

"A Murder, a Mystery, and a Marriage" (1876)

"The Canvasser's Tale" (1876)

"The Invalid's Story" (1877)

"The Great Revolution in Pitcairn" (1879)

"1601: Conversation, as it was by the Social Fireside, in the Time of the Tudors" (1880)

"The McWilliamses and the Burglar Alarm" (1882)

"The Stolen White Elephant" (1882)

"Luck" (1891)

"Those Extraordinary Twins" (1892)

"The Esquimau Maiden's Romance" (1893)

"The Million Pound Bank Note" (1893)

"The Man That Corrupted Hadleyburg" (1900)

"A Double Barrelled Detective Story" (1902)

"A Dog's Tale" (1904)

"The War Prayer" (1905)

"Hunting the Deceitful Turkey" (1906)

"A Fable" (1909)

"Captain Stormfield's Visit to Heaven" (1909)

"My Platonic Sweetheart" (1912, posthumous)

"The Purloining of Prince Oleomargarine" (2017, posthumous)

COLLECTIONS

SHORT STORY COLLECTIONS

The Celebrated Jumping Frog of Calaveras County and Other Sketches (1867), short story collection

Mark Twain's (Burlesque) Autobiography and First Romance (1871), short story collection

Sketches New and Old (1875), short story collection

A True Story and the Recent Carnival of Crime (1877), short story collection

Punch, Brothers, Punch! and Other Sketches (1878), short story collection

Mark Twain's Library of Humor (1888), short story collection

Merry Tales (1892), short story collection

The £1,000,000 Bank Note and Other New Stories (1893), short story collection

The $30,000 Bequest and Other Stories (1906), short story collection

The Curious Republic of Gondour and Other Whimsical Sketches (1919, posthumous), short story collection

The Washoe Giant in San Francisco (1938, posthumous), short story collection

Mark Twain's Fables of Man (1972, posthumous), short story collection

ESSAY COLLECTIONS

Memoranda (1870-1871), essay collection from Galaxy

How to Tell a Story and other Essays (1897)

Europe and Elsewhere (1923, posthumous), edited by Albert Bigelow Paine

Letters from the Earth (1962, posthumous)

A Pen Warmed Up In Hell (1972, posthumous)

The Bible According to Mark Twain (1996, posthumous)

ESSAYS

"On the Decay of the Art of Lying" (1880)

"The Awful German Language" (1880)

"Advice to Youth" (1882)

"Fenimore Cooper's Literary Offenses" (1895)

"English As She Is Taught" (1887)

"Concerning the Jews" (1898)

"A Salutation Speech From the Nineteenth Century to the Twentieth" (1900)

"To the Person Sitting in Darkness" (1901)

"To My Missionary Critics" (1901)

"Edmund Burke on Croker and Tammany" (1901)

"What Is Man?" (1906)

"Christian Science" (1907)

"Queen Victoria's Jubilee" (1910)

"The United States of Lyncherdom" (1923, posthumous)

NON-FICTION

The Innocents Abroad (1869), travel

Roughing It (1872), travel

Old Times on the Mississippi (1876), travel

A Tramp Abroad (1880), travel

Life on the Mississippi (1883), travel

Following the Equator (sometimes titled "More Tramps Abroad") (1897), travel

Is Shakespeare Dead? (1909)

Moments with Mark Twain (1920, posthumous)

Mark Twain's Notebook (1935, posthumous)

Letters from Hawaii (letters written in 1866, published as a book in 1947)

OTHER WRITINGS

Is He Dead? (1898), play

"The Battle Hymn of the Republic, Updated" (1901), satirical lyric

King Leopold's Soliloquy (1905), satire

"Little Bessie Would Assist Providence" (1908), poem

Slovenly Peter (1935, posthumous), children's book

"Some Thoughts on the Science of Onanism" (1879), a speech given to The Stomach Club.

AUTOBIOGRAPHY AND LETTERS

Mark Twain's Autobiography

Chapters from My Autobiography published by North American Review (1906–1907)

Posthumous edition compiled and edited by Albert Bigelow Paine (1924)

Posthumous edition named Mark Twain in Eruption compiled and edited by Bernard DeVoto (1940)

Posthumous edition compiled and edited by Charles Neider

Posthumous edition compiled and edited by Harriet Elinor Smith and the Mark Twain Project: Volume 1 (2010)

Posthumous edition compiled and edited by Robert Hirst and the Mark Twain Project: Volume 2 (2013)

Posthumous edition compiled and edited by Harriet Elinor Smith and the Mark Twain Project: Volume 3 (2015)

Mark Twain's Letters, 1853–1880 (2010, posthumous)

"Territorial Enterprise letters" being compiled for release in 2017

CPSIA information can be obtained
at www.ICGtesting.com
Printed in the USA
BVHW030923300720
585023BV00006B/66

9 789390 027170